THE GRUMP AND THE WRITER

GRUMPY HOT MOUNTAIN MEN
BOOK 2

WENDY ASHFORD

Edited by
STACI FRENES

For my Family

1

ISAAC

The smell of sawdust fills my nostrils as I sip my coffee and stare at the table in front of me. I poured my soul into carving every single inch of it, using different woods with different colors to create the intricate rose pattern the client wanted.

It took me two months to finish it, setting aside other projects I had planned, but it was a challenge I couldn't pass up. It's the most amazing feeling creating something one-of-a-kind that no one has ever seen.

A shaft of sunlight filters through the window, hitting the surface of the table and giving it a warm golden color. It's like an omen: after months of snow and then rain, summer is almost here and the weather is warming up, just in time for this piece to find its new home.

I put down my coffee cup and grab the cloth I use to polish it, starting from the corner and wiping along the edge, enjoying the smoothness of the wood surface.

"I don't think you can make it any more perfect than that." Her voice reaches my ears just a few seconds before her sweet perfume fills my nostrils.

A long time ago, I loved that smell lingering on my sheets. Now, it's just a reminder of my mistake of blindly following my heart. I look up at the figure in the doorway. She looks beautiful, as usual, with her long blond hair, slender figure, and big, innocent blue eyes. But there is nothing innocent about my ex. There's just the elegant appearance and the facade she maintains as the wife of the mayor of this small community.

"What do you want, Elise?" My voice comes out gruff. I don't have many opportunities to talk with other human beings, other than trips to the grocery store or with customers that come into my shop. Most of the contact with my clients is through email.

"Checking if the table is ready for delivery." She smiles at me as she walks further into the shop.

Her elegant blue suit is a stark contrast against

the sawdust covering this place and my plain white T-shirt, jeans, and boots. The click of her heels on the concrete gets on my nerves. It reminds me of how much she changed after dumping me for a better option.

"Like I told your husband yesterday, I've already arranged for the delivery guys to come by this afternoon to pick it up. You didn't need to come all this way so early in the morning," I grumble.

She leans her hip against the table and smiles. "I wanted to be sure everything is fine." Her sugary-sweet voice makes me want to scream.

She is so good at manipulating people, I'm not surprised she has everyone fooled into believing she's the sweet caring wife that has this community's best interests at heart. She fooled me once, too, and I was sure I was way too smart to be taken advantage of.

"You know everything is more than fine, so what do you really want from me, Elise?" I look her straight in the eyes and I don't miss the flash of annoyance crossing her gaze.

She doesn't like to be called out, but I honestly don't care anymore what she thinks about me or if I hurt her feelings. She lost the chance for me to care about her a long time ago.

She walks around the table and puts a hand on my chest. "You always did have a way with your hands, Isaac," she whispers, her breath warm against my ear. "Such skill and finesse. It's...enticing."

Her words send a shiver down my spine, and not in a pleasant way. Immediately after the split, I would have had a hard time fighting the temptation of having her so near, no matter how many red flags were waving in front of my face. But now, all my love for her has changed to resentment, if not hatred.

"Elise," I begin, grabbing her hand and placing it on the table, "we broke up for a reason. Let's not go down that road again."

Over the years, she's come back from time to time, when her marriage was unsatisfying, but never once has she expressed regret for dumping me and treating me like trash, and that, for me, is a major turnoff. Besides the fact that I don't fuck married women.

She leans back, her smile fading slightly as a veil of disappointment settles over her features. She quickly regains her composure, attempting to play it cool. "I know we've had our differences, Isaac," she says and her voice seems almost sincere, "but there's still something between us. Don't you feel it?"

I set down the polishing cloth and step back to

establish boundaries and protect myself. She is good at playing with other people's heads.

"The only thing I feel is betrayal toward your husband."

A flicker of anger flashes across her face, her eyes betraying her true feelings toward me. She just wants a good fuck, not true love, from a woodworker like me.

She steps back and walks toward the door again, stopping in front of the work bench where all my tools are lined up. She touches a chisel with her long fingers and beige manicured nails.

"You know what? I'm offering you some human contact here. I guess you'd rather die alone and miserable," she says without even looking me in the eyes.

I feel the anger boil in my stomach, leaving a bad taste in my mouth. She has some nerve coming here when her husband doesn't satisfy her. And considering she's just looking for sex, I can only assume where he falls short.

"Alone and miserable? You weren't so worried about that when you dumped me, breaking my heart, to marry someone that could give you more money and power."

Power. If I think about it, I want to laugh. We live

in Pinecreek, not exactly a bustling metropolis where the mayor is some kind of celebrity. Poor Albert, having to deal with the fair committee going wild with a proposal that's way over budget, or some unruly tourist causing some commotion before packing and going back to their city. Not exactly worth mentioning in the news, but still. She chose the more influential man between the two of us.

Mayor beats woodworker, hands down, even in Pinecreek.

"It was a difficult choice for me too," she insists, barely turning around to look at me over her shoulder.

"No. It really wasn't. I asked you to marry me and you said no because I have nothing to offer you. Then you got engaged two weeks later to a man thirty years older than you that obviously has what you're looking for in a man." Money and status. But I don't say that. She already knows why she married him.

"That's what you want to see," she says, turning around and walking out the front door.

I let out a long sigh when I hear the engine of her SUV turn on and the crunch of gravel under her tires as she drives down the road away from my house.

I really didn't need this shit right now. I just wanted to enjoy this day and deliver a piece of furniture that brought back dead memories that I didn't want to revive. It was a suffocating two months. I debated for a long time, when Albert came here to commission this piece of furniture, whether to accept the job or not.

I don't have anything against him. He just found himself in the middle of Elise's scheming and he fell for the wrong woman, like I did a long time ago. I don't blame him for the end of our story. She's to blame, and me, too, because I didn't recognize that she didn't love me. She just wanted someone to warm her bed while looking for someone to sink her teeth into.

I grab my cup of, by now, cold coffee and walk out the back door leading to my backyard—or at least what should be my backyard, considering the tall trees that surround this place.

I take a deep breath of the crisp morning air and enjoy the view of the forest that extends behind my house. I'd like to enjoy it, that is, but there is a huge truck parked in front of my neighbor's property. Since old Jack died two years ago, it has stayed empty because his nephews fought over the property. Should they sell it? Should they live in it?

Everyone had differing opinions and couldn't agree on what to do with it.

I got used to not having anyone bothering me here. Living five minutes away from Main Street gives me a chance to enjoy the solitude and quiet I crave during the day. Quiet from a human standpoint, anyway. Around here, there are plenty of birds chirping and other animals rustling in the brush.

Someone comes out of my neighbor's house to grab some tools in the truck and then goes back inside. They must be renovating the house. My stomach tightens even more than when my ex left. Damn. This day is going from bad to worse.

I go back inside, pick up my keys and leave, closing the door behind me. I'm going to take a drive to see the only person I know that will have some answers for me. The source of all Pinecreek gossip: Henry, the owner of the only grocery store in town.

∼

"LOOK WHO WE HAVE HERE! I thought you died in that woodshop." He laughs in his usual friendly way.

Sometimes, I'll wait for days before coming here to buy what I need because I can't deal with his over-the-top friendliness. Don't get me wrong, he is a nice old man, but sometimes he's way too cheery, encouraging, and overly protective with his customers.

He's been here since forever, like his father before him. And this town is so small that everybody knows everybody and you can't have a freaking private life without them all weighing in on your decisions. Or, in my case, taking sides when a couple breaks up.

Henry was so invested in my breakup that Elise and Albert couldn't even come in this place for over a year, until I told him that he can't keep the mayor off the premises, even if his wife is a bitch. Fortunately, Albert was more than understanding and took his stubbornness graciously.

"You must have real faith in my survival skills... or my ability to handle the sharp tools I work with," I grumble sarcastically, grabbing the beer I've put off buying for two weeks. I also grab a bag of chips and some pretzels to go with it.

I put everything on the counter and resist the temptation to roll my eyes when I see his arms crossed over his chest and the smug smile on his face.

"So?" he asks and I frown.

"So what?"

"Are you going to ask me?"

"Ask you what?" I'm genuinely lost here.

"About the truck parked in old Jack's front yard." He grins at me.

Jesus. I came here exactly for this information but I didn't know he was waiting for me to come and ask about that very thing. Sometimes I don't know if I'm too predictable or if he does nothing but stick his nose into other people's business.

"How do you even know I came here to ask you that? It's barely nine-thirty."

"Because they were here asking for information two hours ago and I knew you would have some questions on the matter." He beams like this is his only goal in life, anticipating other people's moves.

"And *do* you know what they are doing?"

"I'm glad you asked. Yes, I do." He grins.

I fight to roll my eyes out of respect for this man, even if I just want to turn around and walk out the door. "Do you want to tell me?"

"They're renovating."

I wait for a more detailed explanation, but he doesn't say anything more.

"I know they're renovating. I can see that for myself. Do you know if they sold the property?" I'm itching to know if I have to deal with a new neighbor.

He shakes his head and I don't know if I'm happy about that or not. Why are they renovating?

"They couldn't agree on whether to sell or not, so they just decided to renovate it and rent it out to tourists. It will be a vacation property," he says cheerfully, like my life isn't imploding in front of his eyes.

"You're kidding, right?" The disbelief dripping from my words must be obvious because the smile falters on Henry lips.

"Of course I'm not kidding! It's big news, we will have more to offer tourists," he insists.

"Yeah. You're happy because they're not in your backyard blasting music and shouting at all hours of the day and night," I spit a bit too harshly.

Henry frowns. "You are the most grumpy man I have ever met. This means more income for everyone in town. Even you," he points out.

"I sell custom carved furniture. It takes me weeks to make it and nobody is going to buy a coffee table to fly back home."

"Well, you could expand your inventory, carving smaller pieces and putting them up for sale here in my shop. I could find a shelf to put them on and branch out, offering unique handmade souvenirs," he explains, pointing to a corner of the shop as though he's envisioning my products over there. He's probably already figured out how many he can fit in the space.

"You've already thought of everything, haven't you?" I grumble again.

"Well, a man has to think about how to provide for his family. If I can add more things to sell, why not? I think you could also ask the other businesses on Main Street and they would be more than happy to display your work. It's more stuff to offer the tourists coming through." He puffs out his chest like he's proud of this idea.

"You've already asked them, haven't you?"

"Of course I have. Would you have done it yourself?"

He scans my things as he gives me a scolding look that drives away all my willingness to fight him on this.

"No, I wouldn't. Because I value my privacy and I don't want more tourists in town."

"Of course you do. You're so grumpy and antisocial that you stay in that house for weeks on end without talking to a living soul. Do you even remember how to talk?"

"I'm doing it right now, aren't I?" I pay for my

groceries and wave goodbye at him before walking out the door again.

On the ride back to my house, I mull over the news and I can't stop my mood from going from bad to worse. There is nothing good that could come from that house being rented. I want to go talk to those stubborn idiots who own it and shake some sense into them. They live in big cities and don't give a damn about locals that have to put up with the consequences of their choices.

I park in front of the house and go back inside. I feel the urge to go to my kitchen window and look at what they're doing in that damn house. I don't know if I want to know, but in the end, I give in and look out the window.

"A freaking fireplace? Seriously? Do they want those stupid tourists to burn down their house and mine too?"

Could this day get any worse?

2

CHARLOTTE

I stare at the computer screen and want to cry. I reread the scene I wrote, and I don't recognize myself. Did I really write this ugly chapter last night? "He pounced on her like a feral cat in heat?" Seriously? God, I'm amazed that a publisher even gave me a chance ten years ago. This is the worst piece of literature ever written. No matter how much I edit it, it doesn't work.

I find the courage to highlight the entire scene and delete it. It feels like a knife stabbing my chest, but there's nothing salvageable about it.

"Okay. You can do this. You can do this." Maybe listening to my own voice saying it out loud will help me get out of this funk.

I stare intently at the screen, my fingers frozen in

midair, unable to type a word. The blank computer screen taunts me, the cursor blinking relentlessly, as if mocking my inability to conjure up a single coherent sentence. I have been stuck on this scene for what feels like an eternity, and my frustration has reached its peak.

Surrounded by an army of empty coffee cups, I'm sure I look like a caffeine-addicted hermit. My hair stands up in every direction, a wild mess that matches the chaos in my mind. The room reeks of stale coffee and neglected personal hygiene, a potent reminder of my current state.

A heavy sigh escapes my coffee-stained lips. "Come on, I'm a best-selling romance author," I mutter to myself. "I should be able to whip up a steamy love scene with my eyes closed."

But closing my eyes could be dangerous. Sleep has become a distant memory. Who needs sleep when fictional characters demand my attention and scenes refuse to materialize? Apparently, not me.

I look out my tiny studio window and sigh again at the sight of the gray wall on the other side. I miss my house, my cozy home office, and the view of the garden I loved and cared for so much.

As I contemplate my writer's block, a sudden ring from my phone jolts me out of my thoughts. I turn toward the entryway table where I left it and face the mirror on the wall, wincing at my own reflection. It's a horror show—hair unkempt, eyes like a panda from sleep deprivation, and coffee stains adorning my shirt.

Ignoring my appearance, I stumble toward the table and grab the phone. It's the alarm I set for my meeting with Christine, my agent, the one where I have to explain why I haven't written a single chapter since our last encounter. This is becoming a nightmare.

I stumble toward the bathroom and fling open the shower door. I'm not sure a shower can fix my appearance, but at least I don't smell like a two-week-old trash can.

When the water hits my naked skin, I let out a sigh. If I can't write this book, I'm screwed and the deadline looming over me is the last thing I need to write something good.

~

I WALK into the coffeeshop and scan the tables for my agent. Christine is already here, and she waves at me. Her perfectly styled hair and flawlessly applied makeup only emphasize my disheveled state. I didn't have time to make an effort to look decent.

"Charlotte, are you okay?" she asks, her smile fading when she takes in my appearance.

"Define 'okay,'" I reply, my voice strained from disuse. "I've been held hostage by this book. It's like the plot is conspiring against me," I blurt out sitting down in front of her.

Her gaze softens a bit and a sweet smile returns to her face. "You've been here with other books, too, but you managed to come out fine every time. You can do it this time too." She gently reminds me that it's not the first time I've been stuck, always guiding me in the right direction with her suggestions to get over the block.

"You don't understand. It looks like I've been marooned on a deserted island with nothing but my laptop and an endless supply of caffeine."

She chuckles and sips at her coffee. "I was going to ask if you want a latté or something, but it's probably better if I order you a chamomile tea."

"There's no way you can push the deadline with the publisher, is there?" I ask shyly.

It's the second time they've given me more time for this novel, I can't push my luck any further. They were understanding because of my divorce, but it's been ten months now since my husband and I split up, and they won't wait longer. I have to get my act together and do my job.

"No, I can't," she says calmly.

I don't know how she does it. She never loses her temper, finds the positive in every situation, and grounds me with her practical suggestions to over-coming my limits. But she can't perform miracles. I came here knowing that she couldn't push the dead-line back. And maybe I came just for that, to remind myself that I can't wait any longer to find the motiva-tion to put on my big-girl pants and finish this book.

"So, two months. That's it." I sigh.

She nods and studies me with her rich brown eyes.

"These characters are driving me insane. They won't cooperate with my plans!" I complain.

"Maybe it's time to shake things up. Throw a curveball their way. Have your heroine elope with the villain or make the hero develop a sudden obses-sion with gardening. Or maybe *you* should change scenarios. Move out of the city for a month or two and find some new inspiration." She smiles at me like it's the perfect response.

"What? I can't go out of town. That's insane!"

"Why? What do you have here? You live in a

studio that is sucking the soul out of you. You cut ties with all your friends years ago because of your ex-husband. It's a couple of months, I'm not telling you to move away permanently. Shake things up, for you *and* your characters!"

I can't argue with her reasoning, but I'm not brave like her. My life is made up of reassuring routines that make me comfortable. I don't like to step out of my comfort zone and the thought alone makes me anxious.

And this is why my husband left me. I became boring and predictable and he decided to live his life without me.

"Am I that boring?" I whisper under my breath.

It's not a question meant for her, but she is always the anchor who keeps me grounded in reality.

"No, you are not, but you have writer's block and an approaching deadline. And those two things are blocking you from delivering the next bestseller. You can stay here and keep telling yourself you are fine inside that tiny apartment, or you can go away for a few months to a place you really like, and do what you know how to do best," she says calmly, like it's perfectly clear to her what I should do. And maybe it is, because she's not living this situation.

I want to be the kind of person who can follow her suggestions blindly, but I'm too much of an over-thinker to do that. My list of "what ifs" is so long I lost count of how many excuses I have to justify sitting still and waiting.

"I will think about it," I concede, but I can see in her eyes she is not convinced.

I don't blame her. I wasn't convinced by my tone either.

~

I OPEN the front door of my apartment, and a sense of dread fills me. I hate this place, with its light grey walls, pale wood furniture, and lack of personality. The view from my previous office was magnificent, with the wildflowers I spent years growing and the bees and butterflies all feasting on that colorful canvas. And then there were the plants I had inside, covering half of the space and giving me the peace I needed to sit and write. But my husband took away that too. He managed to make me walk out of that place with only one bag of clothes, insisting we had to split everything, plants included.

I should have listened to my mom when she told me to make him sign a prenup. I was the breadwinner during our entire relationship, after all. But I was in love, and he convinced me it wasn't necessary because he had no reason to leave me. It turned out that being more successful than him was a deal-breaker for him. He doesn't want my money, not every penny, anyway. He wants to see me fail. He wants to see me crumble into pieces, and he's doing a good job of it.

I put my purse on the coffee table and my eyes land on the brown envelope containing the terms of our divorce. He wants to sell the house. I offered to buy his part, but he won't listen. He knows I carry a lot of memories in that house and that it's the only place that inspires me to write. Unfortunately, we each own fifty percent of the house, and he wouldn't sell it to me even if I paid him ten times what it's worth. I know because I tried.

He wants to get rid of everything that makes me happy.

I wonder when he became so bitter about our relationship. He always joked about my success in a playful way—at least in the beginning. Then, his anger toward my increasing book sales and popularity grew into something ugly. I hate how we fought toward the end of our relationship. I don't mourn him or our marriage, but I sure mourn the happy moments we spent together. Because, at one point, we were happy.

I let out a long sigh and walk to the kitchen to prepare something to drink. I stare at the coffee machine for a long time but then decide to follow Christine's advice and make a cup of chamomile tea. I won't write a single word if I'm sleep deprived and in a bad mood, so I drink the hot concoction and go to bed.

~

I WAKE up at four in the morning, feeling rested and relaxed. I contemplate the idea of staying under the blanket until later, but after tossing and turning for half an hour, I decide to give up and start my day. It's not like I have time to waste anyway.

I walk to the kitchen and prepare a cup of coffee. My healthy habit of decaffeinated drinks of choice lasted less than twenty-four hours. I dig into the pantry, fishing out a couple of chocolate chip cook-ies, considering I didn't have dinner last night.

I contemplate the idea of sitting on the couch and finishing my breakfast, but I hate staring at that grey wall. So I walk into the only room where I get small glimpse of the city between two buildings: my bathroom.

Perched on the lid of the toilet, I watch the city come alive sipping my coffee and nibbling on the cookies.

"What the heck am I doing in this place?" I look around at the bathroom and feel like the biggest loser in the world. "Giving my ex-husband exactly what he wants," I murmur.

I stand up, leave the bathroom, sit in front of my computer, and instead of writing my book, I search for a place to spend the next two months. I won't miss this place even one single minute.

3

ISAAC

It's starting.

My nightmare about having an unwanted neighbor materialized way too soon: it's been less than one week since I saw the truck parked in front of the house. They sure didn't wait for summer to start renting it out.

Yesterday, around seven in the evening, I saw a rental car parked in front of the house, and this morning, when I woke up, there were already lights on. But what annoys me the most is the woman on the front porch typing on her computer. Why would you come to a place like this on vacation if you just want to spend the day in front of your computer instead of enjoying the surroundings? We're in the middle of one of the most scenic areas in the country and she decides to stare at her thirteen inches of screen instead?

"Tourists," I grumble while sipping my coffee.

It's not even seven in the morning, why is she up so early? To type on her computer instead of enjoying the sound and sights of the forest awakening? She should have stayed home and not wasted her money on this place. I was just fine without anyone around.

As soon as the thought crosses my mind, I realize that I'm complaining like those old dudes who are annoyed by everything. I don't like to make a habit of assuming things about people I don't know. If I've learned anything from past experience, it's to mind my own business.

But this time, I can't ignore the fact that this situation is driving me crazy. I always had a great relationship with the old owner, but it took some time to get used to him. Now, I'll have to watch people coming and going every week, different faces, different cars, habits, and everything that comes with that.

I hope they don't expect me to make conversation because I hate small talk. I'd rather stab my fingers with a knife than talk about the weather. 'Yes, it rains a lot. You are in the Olympic Peninsula, what did you expect?' It's always the same questions, and frankly, I'm tired of answering them.

I keep sipping my coffee, staring at the person still seated on the patio. I hope she doesn't think I'm a creepy dude spying on her, but for fifteen years, every morning, rain or shine, I've been having my coffee over here. If she has a problem with that, I'll tell her to go somewhere else.

"Why am I thinking stuff like this?" I murmur to myself, realizing that I'm getting way ahead of the situation. She doesn't even notice I'm here, for Pete's sake.

I sip the last drip of coffee and stand up to go back inside. As I'm rinsing my cup and about to put it in the dishwasher, a bloodcurdling scream comes from outside.

"What the..." I look out the window, trying to see what's happening, but I can't see the woman from here.

Running back outside, I find her standing on the bench where she'd been sitting earlier, still screaming her lungs out. She is a petite brunette wrapped in a lot of layers of fabric and comfy red boots. She looks like she's dressed for the North Pole.

I shake my head, diverting my attention from

her appearance, and run down to her to see what all the fuss is about. I reach the front porch and approach her, but she doesn't notice me and keeps screaming.

"What happened? Why are you screeching like a dying pig?" I ask above her screams.

I obviously startle her, because she turns around so fast she almost topples off the bench. I reach out to help her, but she looks possessed as she jumps into my arms, climbing me like a tree.

"What the hell are you doing?" I shout, trying to put her down, but for a tiny little thing, she's stronger than I expected.

"Get it away from me!" she screeches again, pointing at a spot under the grill on the patio.

I almost laugh. "It's a raccoon," I tell her, hoping to calm her down.

"I know that, but he's hissing at me." Her voice trembles.

I look at the poor guy with his tiny hands still wrapped around a paper towel with what looks like pizza in it.

"Of course he's hissing, you're shouting like a maniac," I point out. "He's scared out of his mind."

She turns around with a frown on her face. She has the most beautiful big blue eyes I have ever seen, with small golden circles in the centers around her pupils.

"He tried to attack me. What if he has rabies?" she says, now annoyed and sounding almost angry.

I scoff, managing to piss her off even more. "I doubt he was attacking you. He's scavenging for food. And we haven't had a case of rabies in raccoon in years, thanks to the vaccine baits. You should be more scared about bats. Those are increasing throughout the Pacific Northwest."

She raises her chin, trying to prove her point. "Well, first of all, I don't know that; second, how can I be sure he isn't aggressive?"

"Well, miss *know-it-all*, first, if you visit a place, you should be aware of the basics of where you are. This is the Pacific Northwest; there is wildlife here. Second, he is hiding behind the grill, can't you see he's terrified? And third, can you please get off me? I'm not your personal climbing tree," I point out with more than a bit of annoyance in my voice.

That last part seems to shake her out of her maniac episode. She looks down, finally noticing she has climbed onto my lap. Her cheeks turn a light shade of pink as she hurries to scramble down. She murmurs a "sorry" under her breath but she doesn't look me in the eyes while doing it. I don't know if she is embarrassed because she jumped on me or because she realized that she overreacted to the whole thing.

I walk around the table where her computer is still open, and I grab the grill. As soon as I move it, the little guy stumbles off of the porch for dear life. He was so terrified he even peed himself. All because of a screaming woman.

"Don't leave food scraps outside, or they will come looking for food," I tell her.

When I face her, she is pouting with her arms crossed over her chest. She has a beautiful face, even with that scowl.

"Do they come this close very often?" she asks stiffly, like she just realized that this is not the city she is used too. Because there is no doubt in my mind she is from the city.

I shrug. "Not if you're around making noise or something like that, but if they learn you leave food outside, they'll come during the night."

She seems more pissed than scared now. "Nobody told me that when I rented this place. It should at least be on the website, so people can be prepared."

My annoyance, which disappeared while freeing the raccoon, comes back with a vengeance. "Well, people *come* prepared, usually, because they choose the location of their vacation carefully, and they do some research *before* visiting a place," I point out with a bit of venom in my voice. Who does she think she is?

She opens her mouth, clearly outraged by the implications of my words. "Well, I did research this place, but I found nothing about wildlife attacking people in their own homes."

You have got to be kidding me. Are these the kind of people I have to deal with for the rest of my life? I can't do this.

"Well, you can always go back to the city you came from and write a bad review of this place. Nobody's stopping you. And since you were already engrossed in your computer this morning, you don't have to change what you were already doing," I spit.

She scoffs. "You have some nerve. You know nothing about me, but here you are, judging my life like you have every right to do so. Who do you think you are?"

I feel my stomach clench with anger. "I'm the one who has to put up with you screaming your lungs out because you don't know the first thing about living in the mountains!" I fight back.

"It was an honest mistake!" she shouts shaking her head like I don't understand what she is saying.

"Whatever," I say turning around and stalking toward my house. I don't want to fight with her anymore. It's useless and I have work to do.

Next time she screams, I'll let her deal with whatever her problem is.

"Unbelievable," I hear her murmur under her breath.

Yes, unbelievable. Why do I feel like my nightmare is just beginning?

4

CHARLOTTE

I walk down Main Street and take a look around. There are not many places to go in Pinecreeck, but this is why I chose this small town in the first place: there are no distractions. It has the essentials, like a diner, a pub, and a grocery store. I need to write a book, not take a vacation somewhere exotic.

I walk into the grocery store, and I'm greeted by the smile of a man in his sixties, maybe, with kind eyes and a friendly demeanor.

"Good morning, dear! How may I help you?" he asks warmly.

"Good morning. I don't know how to explain what I want, but I'll try," I confess, and I feel like an idiot. I'm a writer, for Pete's sake. My job is to explain things to people.

"Let's try." He leans against the counter and smiles.

"I have a raccoon problem." I feel my cheeks go up in flame when I remember how I literally climbed on my neighbor like he was a tree. I mean, he is built like one, with his massive legs, arms...and those pecs. A gorgeous tree, if I'm being honest. But still, I can't go around jumping in strangers' arms.

The man's face falls, and his brows furrow in a grey bushy frown. Now I'm worried.

"Are they inside the house?" He sounds concerned.

"No! They're outside. Can they come inside?" I ask, worried.

My grumpy neighbor's words about researching the place before packing my things and moving come back to my mind. He's right; I should have done some research about the wildlife before coming here. But I will never admit it to him.

Fortunately, the calm expression comes back to the man's face. "Not if you're careful to keep doors and windows closed when you're not in the house. And throw away the trash in the bin down the street sooner rather than later," he reassures me. Or, he tries, at least, because there's a chance that they will come in the house if I'm not paying attention. And focusing on menial tasks is not something I'm good at when I'm deep in writing mode.

"Is there something I can put around the house to keep them away?" I hope he has a solution for keeping them far from my open doors and forgotten windows.

"A repellent?" His eyebrows shoot up.

Repellent! That's the word I was looking for. My author ego takes a blow at my inability to find the correct term.

"Yes, something I can spread around the house."

"We don't keep chemicals here in town for this kind of thing. If I have to be honest, I quite dislike them because they seep into what we eat, into the water, and then poisons us. But you can make a natural concoction," he suggests.

"I'll need help with that." I smile, following him as he walks around the counter and proceeds to pick out a few products from the shelves.

When we go back to the register, I have more doubts than when I came into this place. "Do I really need all these things?"

"The smellier, the better." He chuckles.

I take a look at the onion, jalapeno, garlic,

cayenne pepper, and dish soap and wonder if I have to scare the raccoons or feed them.

"Boil the onion, jalapeno, and garlic for at least fifteen minutes. Then, take out the solid bits, add a good spoonful or two of cayenne pepper and one of dish soap, and then spray it around the house. Or wherever the raccoons tend to gather. If it rains, you'll have to reapply it," he explains.

My house will smell like a trash bin for a few days, but I hope it will help me.

"Thank you," I say.

"No problem. And if you have any trouble, you can always call Isaac, your neighbor, and he'll help." He winks at me.

"How do you know where I'm staying?" I'm curious more than worried. He seems harmless.

"There aren't many places you can rent here in town, and the only one that's a single house where raccoons can feast is next to Isaac's home," he explains.

So, that is the name of my grumpy pain in the butt. "Lucky me!" I murmur, and a smile appears on his face.

"You already met Isaac, did you?" He chuckles.

"How do you know?" I smile.

"Because he's the only one who could piss off a person in just one meeting. It's like his superpower."

I laugh and get the impression he knows him well. "Yes, that's the one."

He smiles at me. "Be patient with him. He is grumpy, but he's a good man. He wouldn't hurt a fly."

I suppose I should trust his word, considering he knows him better than me, but the first impression was not a good one.

~

IF THE RACCOONS don't stay away from the patio, they sure will stay away from me. The smell coming out of the boiling pot on my stove is so strong my eyes water. I have no idea how I will live in this house for two months if I can't keep the windows open and this concoction on the stove. I should have chosen a less wild place to stay.

"Pack your bags and go for an adventure," Christine said. Well, I'm not cut out for adventures.

When I finally manage to put all the ingredients in the spray bottle, I almost faint.

"I'll find dead raccoons all around the house, and they'll charge me with animal cruelty," I murmur to myself while I open the door and peek out to see if there are any furry friends out there.

It takes me a while to spray the front porch, and when I reach the side of the house to start with the bins, I let out a scream when I hear rustling behind me. I turn around, and without thinking, I spray in front of me.

"What the heck..." The booming voice of my neighbor, Isaac, startles me.

"Can you please not jump out of the bushes like a psycho?" I ask, more scared than irritated.

He is waving his hands in front of him with a frown, showing his disgust. "What are you doing?" he barks.

"Spraying a repellent for the raccoons," I answer, annoyed by his tone.

His jaw sets, and his lips tighten in an angry expression. Now that I look at him without panicking, he has gorgeous features. He has long brown hair, a small scar on his bushy eyebrow, a thick beard covering his face, and two deep, brown eyes. Three small moles dot his upper right cheek, just under the corner of his eye—a line that almost resembles a constellation.

He scoffs. "Of course, you come here from your pampered life in the city and take possession of the place, spraying chemicals around our mountains. But who cares, right? You're going back in, what, a week? So you don't have to deal with the consequences."

The annoyance I felt a minute ago is fast becoming full-on anger. Who does he think he is?

"It's all natural, you dumbass!" I spit back.

He seems to be taken aback. "Dumbass?"

"Yes, because you blab about things you don't know without asking," I remark.

"You think it's natural because they put a colorful label on it, but it's not," he insists.

"I literally just boiled the water inside that kitchen and put it into this spray bottle," I almost shout.

He makes a surprised face, and this annoys me even more. Does he think I'm not capable of doing this?

"What did you put in it?" There is a veiled curiosity in his tone.

I take a deep breath, regretting it immediately because the stink is unbearable. "Onion, garlic, jalapeno, cayenne pepper, and a spoonful of dish soap." Saying it out loud sounds even worse.

He scrunches his face and grabs his flannel shirt,

smelling where I sprayed him. "Jesus, that's why it stinks so much. Who the hell gave you that recipe?"

"The guy at the grocery store."

He rolls his eyes. "Of course he did."

He seems almost amused by it and I have the feeling that they are both messing with me.

"Why? Doesn't it work?" I ask.

"Oh, yes. Raccoon won't come near this house for months. But it doesn't keep away bears," he explains with a smug smile.

I stare at him for a long time, hoping he will add some sort of explanation or tell me he is messing with me, but he doesn't say another word.

"You are kidding me, right?"

"No, why should I be?" He seems genuinely curious.

"Bears? There are freaking bears?" I raise my voice.

"We are in the Pacific Northwest, what did you expect?" He frowns.

"And they come near the houses?" My heart almost leaps out of my chest.

"Not many, but some of them come to rummage through the bins."

My eyes grow wide, and my mouth hangs open.

This is not the relaxing place to write I was expecting. I want to cry.

"Are you okay?" He seems concerned, maybe because I can feel the blood draining from my face.

"Yes, I'm fine. You can go now that you've saved the world from the evil poisoner." I roll my eyes.

He murmurs something I can't understand, but he turns around and stalks back to his house. And people ask me why I'm still single after the divorce. *He* is the reason why. If these are the only available men around, I'll stay single forever.

～

I'VE ALMOST FINISHED SPRAYING around the house when another rustling comes from the bushes in the front yard. This time, I know it isn't Isaac because I can hear him working in his house. There are noises of hammering and sawing coming from the attached garage.

I'm not staying here to find out what's behind that bush. I've already had enough of this place, and if I hadn't already paid in advance for two months, I would pack my things and go back to Chicago.

I run into the house, and the smell is unbearable, so I grab my laptop and make a run for my grumpy neighbor's house. I knock furiously at the back door, and when he finally comes to open it, he is completely confused. I, on the other hand, am drooling over him. He got rid of his flannel shirt, and the white undershirt sticks to his torso like someone painted it over his sculpted body. He is covered in sawdust, and he's gathered his hair in a man bun. Can this man get any hotter? I hope not, because my publisher will have to move my next book to the erotica section.

"What are you doing here?" he asks, perplexed.

"I need a place to stay," I answer.

He glances over my shoulder with an expression that says, *You have a place to stay!*

"My rental stinks of boiled onion and garlic, and there is something big lurking in the bushes," I explain.

He frowns. "So?"

"I'm staying here with you," I state without hesitation.

It takes him a couple of moments to get rid of the stunned face. "No, you are not." He scowls.

"Do you want me to get attacked by a wild animal?" I cross my arms over my chest and raise my chin.

"Will it make you shut up and disappear?" He

raises an eyebrow, almost contemplating feeding me to the beasts.

"No, I'll just scream louder than you've ever heard someone screaming." I challenge him.

"Still, you can't come in," he reiterates, keeping a hand on the doorjamb and occupying all the space with his massive figure.

I look back. The rustling bushes are still moving, and the smell of the concoction permeates my nostrils to the point that I'm nauseated.

"Please, only until the smell fades a bit. I will throw up if I stay in there," I plead.

If the guy at the grocery store is right, Isaac should help me out. Now is the moment of truth.

He scrunches his nose as if remembering the pungent horror, then he closes his eyes and takes a deep breath.

"Okay, but you stay in the living room and don't even think about coming into the workshop. I don't want you sticking your nose into my sharp tools and bleeding out over my furniture," he says, laying out his rules.

"Jesus. Who do you think I am? Some idiot who lives under a rock?" I'm almost regretting coming here for help. Almost.

"Have you ever done woodwork?" he points out.

"No, but..."

"Stay away from the damn workshop," he growls.

I roll my eyes. "Fine!"

He steps aside and lets me in. I walk past him with a smile on my face, and when I step foot inside, the distinctive smell of burning wood and his masculine scent hit me.

Crap! I will probably need to call my agent about that erotica book.

5

ISAAC

The smell of coffee pulls me out of sleep like an alarm clock without a snooze button. I sit up, rubbing the back of my neck, trying to piece together why the scent of fresh coffee is wafting through my house.

I didn't make coffee last night.

The thought bothers me as I throw my legs over the edge of the bed. My house is dead silent except for the faint hum of the refrigerator in the kitchen. My first instinct is to assume I left the coffee maker on. But no, this isn't the burnt, bitter smell of hours-old coffee. This is fresh. Bold. Inviting.

And completely impossible because I *live alone.*

Heart thumping, I pull on a T-shirt and head down the hall, my bare feet soft against the hardwood floor. I grab the bat I keep in the hall closet and take a couple of deep breaths, ready to confront the intruder. Rounding the corner into the kitchen, I stop in my tracks.

There's a woman sitting at my counter. Not just any woman, the brunette that, as of yesterday, is making my life a lot more...challenging.

She's sitting cross-legged on one of my stools, her hair in a messy knot on top of her head. The ever-present laptop sits open in front of her, her fingers flying across the keyboard. She's so absorbed in whatever she's doing that she doesn't even notice me. A steaming mug of coffee sits dangerously close to the edge of the counter, like she put it there without watching what she was doing.

Now that I study her better, I notice her petite but gorgeous figure. She is beautiful in the most genuine, simple kind of way. She doesn't need fancy dresses or high heels to grab a man's attention. But that's beside the point.

"What the hell are you doing in my kitchen?" I bark, leaning the bat against the wall. Clearly, I don't need it.

She jumps like I've fired a gun, her laptop wobbling as she throws her hands and grabs at her mug to steady it. Her wide eyes meet mine, startled. "Oh my God, you scared me!"

"I scared *you*?" I cross my arms, narrowing my eyes. "Want to explain why you're here, drinking my coffee, at—" I glance at the clock on the microwave, "—seven in the morning?"

She exhales a shaky laugh, sliding her laptop aside. "Okay, don't freak out—"

She bites her lip, and I can't tear my eyes from the plump rosy flesh. It takes me way too much effort to look back into her eyes.

"Too late."

"Right." She gives me an awkward smile and holds her hands up like she's surrendering. "So, yesterday, I realized your living room is... perfect."

"Perfect," I repeat, deadpan.

"For writing," she clarifies, like that makes it any better. "The light, the vibe, the...energy. It's inspiring. All this wood and the smell of sawdust and smoke from the fireplace is better than the expensive candles I light to get into the mood."

She's not making any sense. What the heck is she talking about? Writing mood? Is that even a thing? And writing what?

"Inspiring enough to *break into my house*?"

"I didn't break in!" she protests, lifting her hands higher. "Your door was open!"

I look at the door that faces my backyard, the one that I never lock because we live in Pinecreek, for Pete's sake. Nobody walks into someone's home uninvited. Nobody except her, apparently.

"My *door*—" I cut myself off, pinching the bridge of my nose. This is not how I imagined starting my day. "And you thought, what? 'Oh look, free coffee and Wi-Fi?'"

Her wince tells me she knows how absurd she sounds, but she won't back down from her position. "I didn't steal your coffee. I made it. For both of us, actually."

She gestures toward the coffee machine, and an inviting, hot pitcher of black coffee taunts me. My mouth waters. I'm a sucker for hot coffee in the morning, and I admit it is nice to find it ready to drink without all the fuss to make it. But still, she shouldn't be here. As soon as I find those bastards who rented the house...

"How thoughtful." My voice drips sarcasm.

"I needed to write," she says, her tone softening. "I haven't written anything good in months, and yesterday something clicked. Your living room...it's like magic. I had to come back. It's a deadline thing."

I don't know what she is babbling about.

"Deadline," I repeat. "You're a writer?"

This explains why she is always glued to her computer. Not a tourist, after all.

Her face lights up like I've just handed her a trophy. "Yes!"

Is she always so cheerful? She's so sunny she almost blinds me with her smile. And, also, she talks a lot. I'm used to my beautiful, sacred silence, especially first thing in the morning, before coffee.

"Apparently, also a trespasser," I grumble.

I shouldn't have saved her from that raccoon. This is what happens when you try to be nice and do the right thing. It backfires, and you find yourself stuck with a crazy woman who runs on caffeine and lack of sleep. How do you even deal with someone like her? She's not dangerous, I reason, but she sure isn't the most reliable person in the room. I could be a serial killer, for all she knows, and she barged into my house without a second thought. Talk about lack of self-preservation.

She sighs. "Look, I'm sorry about the whole... showing-up-uninvited thing, but my ex-husband has made it impossible to work at home. He's holding my home office hostage in our divorce."

I feel a jolt of sympathy for her. At least I'm not

the only one with an asshole ex. But the feeling dies immediately when I remember she is invading my privacy.

I stare at her, trying to decide if I'm still asleep and dreaming. She can't be this crazy, right? "So you decided to hijack *my* house because your ex is a jerk?"

"Well," she says, shrugging. "Technically, I just walked in. Your door was open."

"That doesn't mean *welcome*."

Her shoulders slump. "I just need a quiet place to write for a few days. I'll stay in the corner. I won't even breathe loudly."

The pleading in her tone makes me pause. She really is desperate for a place to stay. And she has one! The neighbor's house that I *knew* would be trouble.

"No."

Her hopeful expression falters. "But—"

"Absolutely not."

I don't even know her name; I don't want her here sticking her nose into my life. Even if her ex is a jerk.

She looks at me like I've just canceled Christmas. "I'll buy my own coffee!"

She has the bargaining skills of a five-year-old.

Does she think this is an all-inclusive resort? I don't know where she came from, but she is not entirely in touch with reality.

"That's the least you could do," I deadpan.

We lock eyes, and for a moment, I think I've won. But then her bottom lip trembles—just slightly— and she looks at me like a kicked puppy. I groan.

There are a few things in this world that make me cave in, and one of them is a woman crying. I can't help but do anything to make those tears disappear. Maybe because I saw my mother shed so many tears for my deadbeat father, and watched, powerless, because I was just a kid and didn't know how to help her.

And her ex is a jerk, and I feel like I share this with her.

"Fine. *Fine.* You can stay." Her face lights up, but I hold up a hand. "But only in the living room. No wandering, no bothering me, and no taking over my kitchen," I point out, walking toward the fridge, finally ready to have breakfast.

"Deal!" she says quickly, her grin so bright it's almost blinding.

I shake my head and turn to the stove, cracking eggs into a pan. I'm halfway through making breakfast when I realize she's still sitting at the counter, sipping her coffee. She's staring intently at me with an expectation in her eyes.

"What now?" I ask, throwing her a look over my shoulder.

"I forgot to eat," she says simply, resting her chin on her hand.

I have no idea how someone can *forget* to eat, but here we are, discovering new things this morning. And I thought it couldn't get any worse.

"Meals aren't part of this arrangement," I grumble, sliding the eggs onto a plate.

"I've been awake since three," she explains, like that somehow makes it okay. "There was a noise outside my bedroom window, and I got scared. Then I found out your door was open—"

She ran over here at three in the morning, and I didn't hear her? I should put a bell on her so at least I know when she sneaks in. And, I have to admit, she is kind of brave, or crazy, I don't know. If I hear a noise outside my bedroom window during the night, I would grab my bear spray, not run out into the woods to my neighbor's house. It's not that far, a few yards at best, but still, a bear is faster than me, even if I run.

"And you thought, 'What's the worst that could happen if I run outside not knowing what is chasing me?' Do you have a death wish?"

She grins, and for the first time, I notice how pretty her smile is. "Well, nothing happened, right? And the man from the store said that raccoons could get into my house. I didn't want to stay there waiting for them to attack me."

I don't point out that bears, too, can break into her house, or she'll be moving in here for however long it takes her to write whatever she is writing.

I grab another plate and shove it toward her. If she's not going to leave, I might as well feed her before she faints or something.

"I'm Charlotte, by the way." She reaches out her hand for me to grab.

Her skin is soft and hot against my calloused fingers, and her hand is so small mine dwarfs hers. But, I admit, I'm a bit surprised by her strong, confident grip.

"Isaac," I grumble.

She smiles brightly at me like I just said something sweet.

As we eat in silence—or at least, I'm silent; she is a chatterbox—I steal a glance at her. She's cheerful, chatty, and completely out of place in my quiet life. She has managed to disrupt my whole routine for the foreseeable future with one single move.

And she's a perfect reminder of why I don't date.

Women like her are too much trouble.

6

CHARLOTTE

I sit cross-legged on the couch, my laptop perched precariously on my knees, but my fingers remain still above the keyboard. The words aren't flowing like they were at three this morning. I should've napped after Isaac caught me here and interrupted my writing spree, instead of diving headfirst into the next chapter. Now, I'm staring at the cursor blinking mockingly at me.

It's a gloomy reminder of how I felt just a week ago, when nothing was coming out of my brain and onto the page. But this time is different. I know there is something I want to say; there is an entire world inside my chest, wanting to come out, but somehow, my mind keeps drifting away from what I should be doing.

The main character in my book is about to confront her love interest in a scene that's supposed to be fiery and emotional. It's one of those intense chapters where you rip your readers' hearts out of their chests, and they'll hate you and thank you for it at the same time. But, every time I try to write it, I'm distracted by the living room around me.

Isaac's furniture is...unexpected.

It's not just that it's sturdy and clearly expensive —it's *beautiful*. The coffee table legs have intricate carvings, subtle but detailed, like someone poured their soul into them. The bookshelf along the far wall is equally impressive. Each shelf is perfectly aligned, and the wood grain seems to shimmer in the sunlight streaming through the window. The shelves look like they were carved into solid wood, following the natural bends and turns of the tree they come from. They're so interconnected that the entire bookshelf seems like one big piece. Rationally, I know it's impossible because it would take a massive tree to make something like this, but no matter how much I try, I can't see where the various parts are joined.

Did Isaac buy these? More than likely, he hired someone to make them for him. It takes an insane amount of time to find the exact pieces to coordinate with the rest of the furniture. He doesn't strike me as someone who spends his days scouring furniture warehouses to decorate his home. Maybe, at some point, there was a woman in his life. Maybe she's still in it, and I feel a bit guilty about barging into her territory like a maniac, even if my intentions are far from romantic.

I never want a man again in my life. One heartbreak in a lifetime is more than enough.

I shake my head, laughing softly to myself. The man doesn't exactly scream *artisanal craftsmanship shopper*. He screams, "Get off my lawn," even when there's no one on it.

He seems more like the type who would *make* those things rather than buy them. I can't help but imagine him hunched over a workbench, carefully sanding a table, or carving those intricate details. My imagination runs wild: Grumpy Isaac in a flannel shirt, sleeves rolled up, sawdust clinging to his forearms...

Oh. *Oh.*

I slam my laptop shut, heat creeping up my neck. Maybe I've been cooped up in here too long. I have definitely lost my mind. I can't be lusting over a man I just met in the spicy-books-I-write kind of way.

Just then, the kitchen door swings open, and

Isaac walks in. His hair is a little messy, like he's been running his hands through it, and he looks at me like he's already regretting whatever words are about to come out of my mouth.

"What?" he grumbles.

"Nothing," I chirp too brightly. He narrows his eyes. Clearly, I'm not fooling him.

I watch as he opens the fridge, his shoulders stiffening. "What's all this?"

"Oh!" I look up, setting my laptop aside. "I stocked the fridge." Or, I mean, I asked the guy from the grocery store to do it and deliver everything to his house. He was quite delighted to find me here.

He turns, holding up a package of deli meat like it's evidence in a trial. "You stocked my fridge."

"Yep. Consider it my way of saying thank you for letting me crash here. I know I kind of—uh—invaded your space."

His face scrunches up in a frown. Jeez, even when he is scowling, he is attractive. He can effortlessly manage that sexy, grumpy lumberjack look that drives women crazy. I usually go for more of a clean face and classy manners in a man, but I have to admit, he's definitely making me explore other sides of my attraction toward men.

"You *definitely* invaded my space."

"Exactly. So, food." I grin like that explains every-thing. I hold my breath, waiting for his reaction, something that tells me he won't kill me on the spot. Suddenly, grocery shopping doesn't seem like such a great idea anymore.

He stares at me for a long moment before muttering, "You didn't have to do that."

I exhale a sigh of relief. "I know. But I wanted to." I expect some kind of reaction from him, but noth-ing. Interacting with Isaac is like bouncing a ball against a wall. Nothing seems to engage him to the point of wanting to have a conversation.

With a low grumble, he pulls out the bread and starts making a sandwich. I'm surprised when, after a minute, he grabs an extra plate and starts assem-bling one for me too. There actually is some softness under that rough exterior, and unexpectedly, I feel the urge to bring it out of him.

"Aw, you *do* care," I tease, resting my chin in my hands as I watch him.

"Don't read too much into it," he says, but his lips twitch like he's fighting a smile.

When he slides the plate across the counter to me, I walk to the kitchen and decide to press my luck. "So, the furniture..."

He arches an eyebrow. "What about it?"

"It's gorgeous," I say, motioning to the coffee table. "The details, the woodwork—it's all amazing. Did you...pick these out yourself?"

He hesitates, his eyes flicking to the table and then back to me. "I made them."

My mouth falls open, a piece of sandwich halfway to my lips. "You *made* them?" When I thought about him bent over a bench, I thought I was just indulging in a fantasy, right out of my spicy romance pages. The fact that it's a reality I never considered unsettles me.

"Don't sound so surprised."

"I just...wouldn't have guessed." I set the sandwich down, my curiosity piqued. "Is that what you do for a living?"

That would explain the smell of sawdust that seems to follow him everywhere. Why didn't I connect the dots sooner?

He nods. His expression is guarded, but then he seems to capitulate and explains. "I run a woodworking business. Custom furniture."

There is no cockiness in his voice, nor does he seem like he's trying to impress me. I mean, most men I know would have talked my ear off, telling me how they patiently carve every piece to perfection. He would have every right to show off his skills; they really are impressive.

"That's incredible." My gaze goes back to the table, seeing it in a new light. "You're really talented."

He shrugs like it's no big deal, but there's a faint flush creeping up his neck. "It's just work."

The way he brushes it off tells me that he doesn't have many people telling him he's good, or at least, the people who matter most. Clients will tell you that they like your work, otherwise, they wouldn't buy it. But sometimes the words or, even better, the actions of the people who love you are more rewarding than a million five-star reviews. If there is anything that my failed marriage has taught me, it's that you can have a bestseller on your hands, but your heart will always listen to the one bad comment from the person you love.

"*Just work?*" I repeat, incredulous. "Nobody puts that much love into something without caring about it."

His eyes meet mine, and for a moment, there's something softer there, something I can't quite place. But, just as quickly, it's gone, replaced by his usual gruffness. I get the feeling he doesn't have many people telling him this, and he doesn't know how to react.

"Why are you asking?" he says, clearly uncomfortable.

There is some kind of wall around his question, like he's ready to shut down this conversation as soon as he feels vulnerable about it. Isaac is a walking contradiction between the love he puts into his work and his icy-cold attitude toward people. He's suddenly become a puzzle I want to figure out.

"I'm fascinated," I admit. "You don't meet a lot of people who can make things like this. Can I see your workshop?"

"No."

The answer is so immediate and firm that it catches me off guard. It's like he slapped the enthusiasm right out of me. I didn't expect a reply so final, even from someone like him.

"Oh," I say, blinking. "Okay. No problem."

He must see something in my expression because he softens slightly. "It's personal," he says, his tone quieter now.

I study him for a brief moment, aware of his concentration on the meal in front of him. I don't think he wants to be rude to people, but he doesn't know how to act around them, either. I feel a pang of guilt for forcing him into a corner.

"I get it," I say quickly, not wanting to push. "I'm

sorry if I overstepped." It's like when I don't want someone to read my first draft. When they ask to do it, I don't want to be rude, but sometimes I don't know how to tell them I don't feel comfortable showing them something that is far from perfect.

He doesn't respond; he just finishes his sandwich in silence.

I focus on my own plate, feeling the shift in the air. I wasn't trying to pry, but it's clear that his workshop—like the furniture itself—is something deeply meaningful to him.

As we sit there, the tension slowly fades, and I catch myself stealing glances at him. There's more to Isaac than the grumpy exterior he wears like armor. Beneath the scowls and grumbles, there's a man who carves beauty out of wood, who pours himself into his work in a way that most people wouldn't bother to. We are more similar than I want to admit.

And for some reason, that thought makes my heart do a little flip.

Which is stupid.

Because he's also the kind of man who would probably rather eat nails than admit he's capable of being kind. He is the kind of man who doesn't express his feelings and bottles everything up until he explodes. Been there, done that, got the T-shirt. I'm not repeating the same mistake again.

"So," I say, breaking the silence. "Do I have to buy my own groceries next time, or is this a one-time pass?" I want to be sure I don't overstep.

He gives me a flat look. "You think you're staying long enough for there to be a *next time*?"

He doesn't know how long it takes to write a book, I guess. He'll be seeing my face for longer than he wants to. For some strange reason, this place gives me the inspiration I need—maybe because of the love he puts into it, and that seeps into the air like a balm for my broken heart. I don't want to give up on my renewed burst of creativity.

I grin, feeling a little braver now. "Who knows? Your door was open once. It could happen again."

He shakes his head, muttering something under his breath, but I catch the faintest hint of a smile. And for now, that feels like a win.

7

ISAAC

As I step into the house, kicking off my boots and brushing sawdust from my hands, the door creaks behind me. The familiar scent of wood and varnish clings to my nostrils, but it's overwhelmed by something warmer —coffee, vanilla, and maybe a hint of lavender. *Her.* It's strange how quickly a person can get used to another, the smell, the laugh, the voice. Now, when I enter my living room, I know I'll get hit with a swarm of questions and chatter.

I'm usually a loner, not comfortable having people around for a long time. I got used to living alone, and I'm not willing to compromise that for anyone. I value my privacy and my habits too much to accommodate another person. Yet, here I am, knowing I'm not alone anymore and not exactly saying no to it.

Fifteen days. That's how long Charlotte's been camped out in my living room, typing away like her life depends on it. And maybe it does. She's here under some half-baked excuse about writer's block and deadlines, but I've stopped questioning it. It's easier to let her stay than argue with her relentless optimism. It's like having a cheerful puppy that is happy when you come home, and maybe I should consider getting one when she's gone. That reminds me that I have no clue about how much longer she'll stay.

I round the corner to the living room, expecting to find her hunched over her laptop like always, but I stop dead in my tracks.

Charlotte is on the couch, her head nearly upside down, one arm awkwardly stretched behind her, and her butt—curvy, distracting, *very* prominent—is sticking straight up in the air. A series of not-so-wholesome thoughts cross my mind, and my cock twitches in my pants. This is new and unexpected, and I honestly don't know if I like it better than when she talks my ears off. The view is a bit unsettling.

"What the hell are you doing?"

She jerks upright with a yelp, nearly toppling off the couch. Her face turns scarlet as she scrambles to sit properly, tugging at her oversized sweater like it can shield her from the absurdity of the moment. It's not like she can erase the embarrassment from her face, which I can see has turned a bright shade of red, even hiding behind that piece of fabric.

"I—uh—." She clears her throat, avoiding my gaze. "I was trying something for my book."

Her voice comes out a bit insecure, and the red on her face deepens. This is the first time I've seen her acting almost shy. She's cute in the most genuine kind of way.

"Trying *what*?" I raise an eyebrow, folding my arms as I lean against the doorframe, enjoying every moment of this conversation. For the first time, I'm the one asking questions, and she's struggling to answer. This is definitely new.

Her blush deepens again. I'm worried she'll burst into flames at this point. "A pose."

I tilt my head, waiting for more. This is becoming funnier by the minute, and it's a pleasant feeling that expands inside my chest. It's not like I encounter absurd situations like this every day of the week. I'm definitely enjoying this.

"You know, to see if it's physically possible," she

mumbles, waving a hand like that explains everything. I'm starting to figure out what she means by a *pose*, and I'm going to milk every ounce of embarrassment out of her this time.

I stare at her, and a slow grin tugs at the corner of my mouth. "Physically possible for *what*, exactly?" I want to hear her say it out loud.

Her eyes snap to mine, wide and horrified. "Oh, God. Not—it's not what you're thinking!"

"Uh-huh." I raise an eyebrow to silently call out her bullshit.

"Okay, it's exactly what you're thinking," she mumbles, and I stifle a laugh.

"Oh, really?" I taunt her.

She huffs, crossing her arms defensively. "It's for a scene. A very specific scene. I'm a writer; this is research."

"Right." I fight back another laugh, but the amusement must show on my face because she groans, burying her face in her hands.

"Don't look at me like that," she mutters.

"Like what?" I tease.

"Like you're judging me."

I'm surprised she thinks I'm judging her. I usually don't give off that kind of vibe.

"I'm not judging," I say, smirking. "Just...observing." And the image of her round ass in the air will be stuck in my mind for a very long, long time. My cock twitches in my pants again, just thinking about it.

She glares at me, but there's no real heat behind it. "Fine. Mock me all you want. It's not like you've never done something ridiculous for your work."

I think about that time I carved a unicorn holding up a dinner table. That was ridiculous, and it took me an insane amount of time to finish it. They paid well, though. Still, I'm not telling her about it.

"Can't say I've ever stuck my ass in the air for it."

Her laughter bursts out before she can stop it, and she quickly covers her mouth, shaking her head. "Okay, fair. But you're a woodworker. Your work doesn't require..." She trails off, her cheeks pink again.

At this point, I'm curious to know what the hell kind of books she writes if *doing research* consists of obscene acts.

"Creative poses?" I chip in, enjoying her embarrassment a little too much.

"Exactly." She clears her throat again, sitting up straighter. "Anyway, now that you've thoroughly humiliated me, I think it's your turn to share. What's the most ridiculous thing you've done for your work?"

She is trying to change the subject and I let her off the hook. "Not much room for ridiculousness in woodworking," I say with a shrug.

"Boring answer." She props her chin on her hand, watching me with a spark of curiosity in her eyes. "What about your most impressive project?"

I would like to say the table that's now in my ex's dining room, but I don't even want to go near a conversation about her. I don't want to deal with her questions and probing.

I'm tempted to deflect, but her curiosity is genuine. "There's a cabin up in the mountains," I admit reluctantly. "Built everything in it. Floor to ceiling, furniture, fixtures—everything."

Her jaw drops, and for some reason, her reaction makes my chest tighten. "That's incredible, Isaac. Seriously."

Her admiration moves something deep inside my chest that I've had buried for I don't even remember how long. With time, my job became my escape, and nobody pays enough attention to really understand the work behind it.

"Yeah, well. It's just wood." I downplay it, not knowing what else to say.

I'm not used to bragging about my work, mostly because I don't think it's a big deal. I'm lucky enough that this kind of thing comes naturally to me. I have always had a knack for manual work, and I have an eye for what the wood calls for. Not every piece of lumber is the same, and not all of it is fit for every kind of furniture. I'm just good at understanding and *listening* to the wood.

"No," she says firmly, sitting forward. "It's not. It's talent and dedication and—"

"Are you always this complimentary?" I cut her off, uncomfortable with the turn in the conversation.

Jesus, I forgot how tiring it is to have a conversation with someone, especially when they can't stop praising me. I don't know how to respond to these compliments.

She grins. "Only when it's deserved."

I shake my head, trying to ignore the warmth her words stir in me. Feelings. This is why I stay away from people. I don't want to be around them because one thing leads to another, and then you find yourself heartbroken and in pieces. Even if she doesn't strike me as the kind of person that walks all over someone's heart.

"So, what kind of books do you write, anyway? Besides ones that involve questionable poses." I try to change the subject, to bring back those pink cheeks that suit her so well.

Her expression brightens. "Spicy romance."

I blink. "Spicy...what?"

"You know. Romance novels with a little extra *heat*." She winks, and I can't decide if she's joking or if she enjoys making me squirm.

I should have known it was something like that. She's so romantically optimistic and sunny that I can't see her writing a horror story. But you never know. When they catch the serial killer, the surprised neighbors always say they were the kind of person that *lights up* the room. Sure, more like an arsonist. Go figure.

"Why am I not surprised?" I mutter.

"Hey!" she protests, laughing. "What's that supposed to mean?"

I hope she's not offended by my comment. It wasn't meant to be judgmental.

"It means you've got the energy for it," I point out, raising my eyebrow to let her know that it should be obvious. She's like a cheerful squirrel on caffeine. And considering the amount of coffee she throws down, the only thing that separates her from the rodent is that she doesn't have fur and she is way, way more attractive.

She tilts her head, amused. "Is that a compliment?"

Why does everything have to be a compliment? It's just a statement, for Pete's sake! "No idea," I grumble.

"Hmm." She studies me, her smile teasing. "Well, if you must know, I'm a *New York Times* bestseller."

I blink, caught off guard. "You're famous?"

This leaves me stunned. Here she is complimenting my work when she's the one reaching the kind of success that very few have achieved. She's so humble about it that I have to admire her for how she's handled herself. The success obviously didn't go to her head. She's not some snobbish woman that takes everything for granted. On the contrary, she looks like a crazy woman who doesn't do things in a calculated way...unlike my ex.

She shrugs. "Define famous."

I don't know if she's serious, but she doesn't look like she's fishing for compliments. "People know your name?" I suggest.

"Some do," she says with a small smile. "I make good money, so I guess that counts for something."

"Huh." I stare at her, taking in the contrast between her casual tone and the weight of what she's just admitted. It's humbling in a way I didn't expect. "Didn't peg you for a bestselling author," I admit with a bit of shame.

"What did you peg me for?" She chuckles, and I know she isn't offended by my words.

"A pain in the ass." My lips curve in the corner with a smug smile.

She laughs. It's a genuine, melodic sound that makes my smirk widen. "Fair enough," she says. "But seriously, it's not all glamorous. Deadlines, stress, people thinking you're one step away from writing porn..." She rolls her eyes.

"Isn't that what you're doing now?" I tease her with a smile.

"Technically, yes," she admits.

I can't help it, and have to laugh.

"Speaking of which," she says, her tone turning playful, "if you're so curious about my work, maybe you should help me with my research."

I freeze, her words hanging in the air between us.

It's a joke. It has to be. But, for a split second, my mind goes places it shouldn't, imagining her perched on the edge of the couch, looking at me like that... and me pounding her from behind. Damn. I can't go there. I can't think about her like that, or I won't be able to stop myself from doing stupid things like kissing her, tasting her, and fucking her on that couch.

I clear my throat, forcing the thought away. "You don't want to poke that bear."

Her smile falters, her cheeks turning a deep shade of red. "Oh."

The air between us shifts, the playful banter giving way to something heavier, more charged. She looks away, fidgeting with the hem of her sweater, and for a moment, I regret saying anything at all.

But I can't let myself go there. Charlotte is a whirlwind, a ray of sunshine that doesn't belong in the shadowy corners of my life. Letting her stay has been a mistake from the start, and yet...

I watch her for a moment longer, the faint blush still coloring her cheeks, and I realize with a sinking feeling that staying away from her is becoming harder by the day.

8

CHARLOTTE

I've been staring at my laptop screen for the past hour, and nothing useful has come to mind. No clever dialogue, steamy banter, or even a coherent sentence. This is the last part of the manuscript, where the reader roots for the couple, and then there is the breakup and the makeup. I've written a billion scenes like this, and nothing. I'm stuck. I slump back into the couch, throwing my hands up. "That's it. I'm going out."

Isaac grunts from the kitchen where he's doing something suspiciously loud with a frying pan. He's been avoiding me ever since the couch pose incident a week ago, which is both irritating and amusing. I really struck a nerve with that suggestion of trying the poses together. I honestly thought he would

laugh at it, but the way he said not to poke the bear
was quite serious. I've wondered many times if he
said it because the thought had already occurred to
him. Because I've certainly thought a lot about
trying out my spicy scenes with him. I'm divorced,
not blind, and there is no way around it: he is
gorgeous in the most delicious way.

I stand up and walk to the stove. I poke my head
around his massive figure and peek at his frowning
face. "Hey, you should come with me."

I don't think that what he is cooking is edible
anyway.

"No." His reply is immediate, flat, and final, like
the slam of a judge's gavel.

I fold my arms. "You don't even know where I'm
going."

This loner part of him is becoming more and
more tiring. Does he do anything for fun? I spend
most of my days in this place, and he's always working. I'm working, too, but at least I take some breaks
from time to time, even if the deadline is looming
over me like a menacing cloud.

"Doesn't matter." He doesn't look up as he flips
whatever's in the pan. "I don't do 'going out.'"

Really? I would have never guessed. I roll my
eyes at his predictability. I can already tell what he's

going to do in the next few hours: he eats in silence and grunts at my questions and then goes back into his workshop for a few "last-minute projects" that come up. I've lost count of how many of those he's discovered since I met him. I suspect he doesn't want to stay near me, so he finds things to keep him busy on the other side of the house, far away from me. And I feel a bit guilty because I know I've completely disrupted his life.

"Well, you do tonight," I declare, grabbing his attention. He finally looks at me, and I seize the opportunity. "I'm serious, Isaac. I need to be around people. If I stare at my laptop or your ceiling for one more hour, I'm going to lose my mind."

"You're already halfway there," he mutters.

If I didn't already know it, he makes it clear he thinks I'm a crazy woman—and maybe I am a bit, considering I just barged into a stranger's life and made myself right at home. I've never done anything like this, but when inspiration strikes, I'm not throwing away the chance to finish my book. Too bad for him that it happened in his house.

I ignore him. "Come on. You have to eat anyway, right? And I'm not cooking tonight. And that doesn't smell or look edible." I point at the half-burned round shape in the pan.

He sighs, turning off the burner. "I don't do people either."

"Well, it's about time you start. What kind of grumpy recluse are you if you won't even show me where the town hermits gather to grumble in unison?"

He pinches the bridge of his nose, muttering something I don't catch. But, after a long pause, he finally says, "Fine. But don't complain if you end up regretting it."

I silently cheer over my victory. It was easier than I expected.

"Regret dinner with my favorite woodworker? Never." I beam at him, and he rolls his eyes, but there's a hint of a smile tugging at the corner of his mouth. He probably knows that he would have to start over making dinner anyway, since the first one didn't go as planned.

~

I'M WAITING in the living room when Isaac steps out of the bathroom after his shower, and the sight of him hits me like a sledgehammer to the senses.

Black ripped jeans hug his long legs, the faded gray T-shirt clings to his chest in a way that should be illegal, and his damp hair is tied back in a care-less man bun that makes him look like some kind of rugged, brooding god. I already knew he was built like a tree, but the loose flannel shirts fooled me into thinking that he wasn't this *well-defined*. His biceps are so huge that I don't think he'll get through the entire dinner without ripping his shirt to shreds. And those abs under that T-shirt? I sure as hell didn't notice those before, or I wouldn't have been struggling to write my book's spicy scenes.

My brain short-circuits.

"Ready?" he asks, grabbing his keys from the counter.

"Uh-huh," I manage, trying to keep my mouth from hanging open.

His boots thud against the hardwood floor as he walks past me, and I'm positive he knows what he's doing. Nobody looks that hot without at least a little self-awareness. Maybe this is why he doesn't go out. He knows he'll kill a couple of women each time just with his mere presence.

"Don't stare too hard," he says dryly, not even glancing back.

"I wasn't staring!" I squeal.

He smirks over his shoulder. "Sure you weren't."

I grumble under my breath, grabbing my purse and following him out the door.

~

ISAAC DRIVES us to *The Twist*, a diner in town that looks like it was ripped straight out of the 1950s. Neon lights buzz softly in the evening air, and the faint hum of music spills out as we walk inside.

"So, what's the deal with this place?" I ask, glancing around.

It's old but new. I don't know how to explain it. It has this familiar vibe, like the old diners where families used to gather for a meal. It's modern-looking, but not impersonal or a tourist trap, as I would have expected. It's like they want their customers to feel like they're a big family. I like it.

"New owner. Some New Yorker who decided Pinecreek would be a perfect place to find love and snatched up the hermit of this town."

"Hmm." I tap my chin, pretending to be deep in thought. "Someone who's more of a hermit than you? Unbelievable."

Isaac gives me a pointed look. "I'm not a hermit."

"Sure you aren't."

We slide into a booth, and I can't help but notice how small the table feels with him sitting across from me. His presence is overwhelming in the best way—broad shoulders, sharp gaze, and that damn man bun that should not be as attractive as it is.

When the waitress comes by, we order the specialty of the day, since Isaac told me they change the menu every day, and I sip my water, trying to gather the courage to ask the question that's been sitting in the back of my mind since day one.

"So," I start, leaning forward. "Why are you single?"

He freezes mid-reach for his drink, his eyes narrowing. "What kind of question is that?"

I know he'll probably close up and avoid answering, but this time he can't run to his workshop. At least, I hope he won't.

"An honest one." I shrug. "Look, I write male characters for a living. Men written by women, no less. And you...well, you check all the right boxes." I wave a hand in front of me, trying to explain what I mean.

"Do I?" He raises an eyebrow, clearly skeptical.

Is he genuinely unaware of his attractiveness? Seriously, he just needs to look in the mirror. Plus, he agreed to go along with my crazy idea of writing in his house. He isn't a bad person at all.

"Yeah. Tall, broody, ridiculously good with his hands..." I trail off, watching his reaction. I like teasing him, especially in public, where he can't turn around and leave. I know I'm a bit of a jerk for doing it, but after weeks of ruminating over this curious fact, I couldn't pass up this chance to ask him about it.

His ears turn pink, and I have to bite back a grin. "I'm not broody."

"Sure you aren't," I tease.

He fights a slight smile that tries to curl his lips. He shakes his head, but there's a flicker of something softer in his expression. "If you must know, I proposed once."

I didn't think he was going to answer like *that*. I knew I had pushed my luck, and I was ready for him to grunt something like, "Mind your own business." But proposing? That requires a hell of a lot of inter-action with another person to get to that point. So, he wasn't always a hermit. A broken heart trans-formed him into one.

I blink, surprised by his honesty. "What happened?"

"She chose someone else." He says it simply, without bitterness, but the weight of those four words hangs in the air between us.

That is a low blow, even for a straight-shooter like him. Now, I understand his reluctance to open up to people. A bruised heart can do that to a person.

"Oh," I say softly. "I'm sorry."

He shrugs, but his gaze is distant. "It was a long time ago."

I want to say something comforting, something profound, but all I can think about is how much I understand what he's feeling. My own marriage might not have ended with betrayal, but the failure still stings. I wondered a lot of times how I could have missed how distant my ex-husband and I had become. I tried to pinpoint the moment we started to drift apart without being able to come up with an answer. I suppose it's the same for Isaac. They were clearly on two different pages.

"I get it," I say finally. "It's hard to put yourself out there again after something like that."

He looks at me, really looks at me, and for a moment, I feel like he sees straight through the sunny facade I've built around myself. The one that sometimes falters when I'm alone, and I let myself be vulnerable.

"Yeah," he says quietly.

I fidget with my napkin, suddenly self-conscious. "The thing is, I write about people overcoming stuff like this all the time. Falling in love again, taking risks...but I can't seem to follow my own advice."

I try to smile, but I can feel that it never reaches my eyes and I can see it in Isaac's furrowed brows.

"Maybe you should try," he says, his tone so matter-of-fact that it catches me off guard.

I glance up at him, confused. "Try what?"

"Like you try your poses." There's a hint of a smirk on his face, but his eyes are serious. "Maybe it'll work."

Heat creeps up my neck, and I'm not sure if it's from embarrassment or something else entirely. "Are you saying I should treat love like...research?"

"Why not?" He leans back in the booth, his arms crossing over his chest. "Seems to work for you."

I laugh, shaking my head. "You're impossible, you know that?"

He shrugs, but there's a ghost of a smile on his lips.

As the waitress drops off our food, I can't help but feel the shift in the air between us. The walls

Isaac's built around himself are still there, sturdy and tall, but for the first time, I can see cracks in them.

And if I'm being honest, I think mine are starting to crack too.

9

CHARLOTTE

I toss my purse onto the small table by the door, kicking off my shoes and sighing with relief as we step into Isaac's house. I should go to my rental, but my computer is here, and I could squeeze in a couple of more hours of writing. Or, maybe just hang out with a surprisingly relaxed Isaac.

Dinner at *The Twist* was unexpectedly delightful. The chef cooks only what is fresh that day, without sticking with a standard menu, and in all honesty, you can taste the difference. It was one of the best meals I've ever had. But now my stomach is full, and my head is swirling with everything the man revealed tonight.

I glance at him as he closes the door behind us,

his shoulders brushing the frame as if he's too big for this space. His man bun is a little looser now, some strands escaping and clinging to his neck. The faded gray shirt from earlier rides up slightly as he stretches his arms above his head, exposing a strip of taut, sun-kissed skin. His lower abs are smattered with dark hair, an inviting sight that disappears under the hem of his jeans.

I feel the heat pooling in my lower belly and my heart picking up speed. It's been a long time since I've even considered being with another man, other than my ex-husband, but Isaac seems to awaken in me that part that screams, "You're a woman, for Pete's sake! Give in to your instincts."

Damn him for looking that good while being oblivious to it.

"You're staring again," he mutters without turning around.

"I wasn't staring." I lie. Badly.

God forbid if I ever have to lie to save my life. I'd be dead the first time I open my mouth. And, considering I make up stories for a living, this pretty much sums up my social skills.

"Sure," he says, his voice dripping with sarcasm as he heads to the kitchen.

I follow him, unable to resist poking the bear a little

more. It's way too easy to tease him. "It's not my fault you decided to clean up tonight. You could've given me some warning, you know. Maybe prepared me for the man bun situation." I wave my hands in his general direction and watch his brows raise in a silent question.

He grabs a glass from the cabinet, his movements slow. "The man bun situation?" He sounds genuinely curious and clueless about what I mean. It's no surprise that he always seems oblivious about his appearance.

"Yeah." I lean against the counter, crossing my arms. "It's unfair. You can't just look like that and expect me to act normal."

I feel my cheeks go up in flame. I may be the one who writes spicy novels, but I definitely do not know how to flirt. God only knows how bad I am at this.

He turns to face me, glass in hand and raises an eyebrow. "You're blaming your lack of self-control on my hair?"

He sounds almost amused by this situation. Maybe he's surprised I'm so straightforward in telling him about my attraction for him, but he doesn't seem to mind it. At least he hasn't run out to his workshop...yet.

"Not just your hair. The jeans, the boots, the

whole lumberjack-meets-rockstar thing you've got going on. It's a lot to process, Isaac."

He lets out a dry chuckle, the corners of his mouth quirking up in that infuriatingly sexy way. "You're ridiculous."

I like that he's taking this conversation as it's intended. It's endearing to watch him navigate this unusual openness toward another person. It's like watching a toddler tentatively explore the world.

"Maybe." I shrug, not even pretending to be offended. "But I'm also right."

He shakes his head, but there's a flicker of amusement in his eyes as he sips his water. I think he likes that I notice him. Maybe he doesn't do it on purpose, but he definitely enjoys that I'm attracted to him.

I watch him for a moment, the silence between us stretching just long enough to feel charged. My heart skips a beat when his gaze flicks to mine, holding it a little longer than necessary. There is a small smile curving his lips, but the thing that really gets me going is the spark of mischief that burns in his eyes. I started this, I poked the bear, and now I almost want him to devour me with that luscious mouth of his.

I clear my throat, desperate to break the tension. "So, you never answered my question earlier."

"What question?"

"Why you think I should 'try' love like I try my poses," I say, air-quoting the word and giving him a teasing smile.

His eyes light up with something very close to lust, but he tamps it down.

He shrugs, leaning back against the counter. "You're not afraid to look ridiculous if it helps you figure something out. Maybe love's the same."

Well, I never thought about it that way. In the beginning, I felt stupid trying something out, even in the privacy of my office, but then I thought, who cares? I'm doing my job, and I'm doing it well. This is research!

I narrow my eyes at him. "Are you suggesting I should approach relationships with the same level of shameless commitment I apply to fictional sex scenes?"

"Maybe." His voice is a little bit raspy, as if this conversation is affecting him too. He has all this grumpiness going on, but the more I spend time with him, the more I think it's just a protective layer he's wrapped around himself to not get hurt. It's like the bark of the trees he has to scrape away to build his furniture. I have to scrape away that layer of grumpiness that keeps people at arm's length.

I laugh, pushing off the counter to stand in front of him. "Well, for your information, Mr. Know-It-All, it's not as easy as it sounds. Sometimes, the poses I write about are physically impossible," I joke.

"Is that so?" His tone is skeptical, but his lips twitch like he's fighting a smile.

Am I really doing this? Luring the bear out of his lair to see what happens? I've never been so brave. Yes, I'm bold when I write those scenes, but reality is an entirely different story.

"Yes, it is." I place my hands on my hips, raising an eyebrow, daring him to challenge me. "Which is why I had to test that pose on the couch the other day."

He exhales sharply through his nose, and for a second, I think he might actually be laughing. "You're unbelievable." His voice is raspy and strained, like it's taking a huge effort to restrain himself.

I don't want him to be restrained. I want him to unleash the animalistic instinct I know is hidden inside him. I glimpse it briefly, trying to crawl its way to the surface.

"And you're curious," I shoot back.

"Curious about what?"

There is a teasing tone in his voice, more than cluelessness. He is daring me to say it out aloud.

"About whether or not the poses are possible," I say, stepping closer. "Admit it."

The heat pooling in my lower belly is like molten lava. The tingling sensation in my core almost makes me squirm. I'm like a landslide, unable to stop tumbling toward the bottom of whatever this is, trampling over everything it comes across. There is no turning back. No casual "Never mind. Just joking!" to escape what I started. And I'm honestly enjoying every second of it.

He shakes his head, but the pink creeping up his neck gives him away. The twitch in his jaw tells me that he's nervous. But he's not backing away. He's not making up excuses about having something else to do.

"You're impossible," he mutters, but doesn't move.

"And you're avoiding the question," I counter, emboldened by the way his gaze dips to my lips before snapping back up to my eyes.

The tension between us is electric, the kind that makes my skin prickle and my pulse race. I don't know who moves first, but suddenly, we're inches apart, the air thick with unspoken desire. I have to tilt my head back to look into his eyes, and what I see almost makes me give in and kiss him. The lust, the desire pooling in those beautiful irises, is a sight that would make any woman cave, and I'm not immune to it. On the contrary, I'm willingly daring him to make a move.

"I already told you. You shouldn't poke the bear," he warns, his voice low and gravelly.

"Maybe I like living dangerously," I whisper, my heart pounding as my gaze flickers on his lips.

For a moment, I think he's going to pull away. His jaw tightens, and his hands clench at his sides as if he's physically restraining himself. But then, something shifts.

With a growl of frustration, he grabs my waist and pulls me against him, his lips crashing onto mine with a force that takes my breath away.

It's not a gentle kiss. It's hungry, desperate, like he's been holding back for too long and finally snapped. I'm surprised and still for a moment, trying to tell my body to do something, anything, but my brain seems to flatline. But when I finally come back to my senses, I kiss him back just as fiercely, my hands tangling in his hair and pulling the man bun loose.

He groans against my mouth, his grip tightening on my hips as he backs me up against the counter. My head spins, and all I can think is how *right* this feels—like we're two puzzle pieces finally snapping into place. My body reacts to his in the most mouth-watering way, like it's coming back to life after a long, uneventful slumber. Was it always supposed to feel this good?

When he pulls back, we're both breathing hard, and his eyes are dark with an intensity that sends a shiver down my spine.

"You're trouble," he mutters, his voice rough.

"You like trouble," I counter, tugging him back down for another kiss.

This time, it's slower, more deliberate, as if he's savoring every second. His hands slide up my sides, brushing the hem of my shirt, and I gasp at the contact. I arch against him and swallow the groan that escapes from his throat. The bulge in his pants speaks volumes. He wants me at least as much as I want him.

"You sure about this?" he asks, his lips grazing my ear.

I don't think I could stop now, even if I dropped dead on the floor. He'd probably resuscitate me just with his touch.

"Yes," I breathe, not a single doubt in my mind.

With that, he lifts me onto the counter, his hands firm but gentle, pushing my knees apart, slipping between them, and pressing his hard length against my wet, wanting opening. There are too many clothes between us, a problem I'm determined to solve sooner rather than later. I don't want to come without feeling his skin against mine, his thick manhood buried deep inside me. I put one of my hands on his shoulders and push myself up, trying to reach the button of my pants in the process.

"Is this one of your poses?" he asks, his tone teasing as he trails kisses down my neck.

"Not even close," I manage, laughing despite myself. "But I'm trying to get rid of these clothes, and I'm stuck."

He pushes back just a little, leaving a soft kiss on the tip of my nose. He studies me with a smug smile on his face.

"Let me give you some material to work with for your book," he says, unbuttoning my pants and dragging them down with my panties in one smooth move, making me squeal while I grab the counter so as not to fall.

He throws my clothes to the side, then he kneels

in front of me, looking up with a mischievous glint
in his eyes.

He takes my breath away.

He peppers my inner thighs with soft, slow
kisses. His beard tickles my skin, and I'm mesmerized by how perfect he is as he makes his way from
my knees up and up until he is almost there. I let out
a frustrated groan when, instead of burying his face
at the top of my legs, he goes back and starts from
the opposite knee, taking his time to perpetuate this
slow, agonizing, mesmerizing torture.

When he finally reaches the desired destination
again, this time he doesn't stop. He looks at me straight
in the eyes and laps his tongue from the bottom of my
opening to the peak where the clit is hot and ready.

I let out a long, deep groan of such pleasure it
makes him smirk between my thighs. He freaking
knows what he is doing. He is a master at this.

He sucks, and nibbles, and laps like his life
depends on it, and when he sinks two thick,
calloused fingers inside my wet opening, bending
them and hitting the right spot, I come harder than I
have ever come in my entire existence.

Oh, those incredible, capable hands!

Wave after wave of undiluted pleasure expands

from deep down in my core to every single cell and nerve in my body. I shake so hard I clench my legs shut, not worried about his head in between them. He chuckles but keeps sucking at my clit, helping me ride this immense orgasm that hits me.

When he stands up, I'm still shaking, but I drag him against me and taste myself on his lips.

He is still way to covered up for my taste.

"I need you inside me, now," I murmur biting the lobe of his ear and making him shiver, tightening the grip of his hands around my waist.

"It's still for research, right?" He chuckles.

"Yes, of course, purely academic." I breathe out, still panting.

His chest rumbles with a low laugh, but he turns around, opens a low drawer in the kitchen, and rummages through it until he pulls out a box of condoms.

He unbuttons his jeans in a slow, deliberate gesture, and when he pulls them down with his boxer briefs, my mouth hangs open like it's the first time I've see a cock. In my defense, I've never dealt with something so massive outside of the pages of my books. I'm hoping this night won't turn out as a thriller, blood and crime scene included.

"Is that how you describe it in your books?" He chuckles, seeing my bewildered expression.

"Better. This is way better. I should take notes." I wink at him.

He doesn't wait for me to recover from my stunned state; he slips between my legs and sinks deep inside me in a slow, relentless motion. He fits tight, and I need a moment to adjust to his size, but when I put my hands around his neck and start to move up and down his shaft, he takes it like an invitation to fuck me thoroughly over this counter. He pushes deep into me with slow, powerful thrusts.

Another orgasm builds inside me with every slap of his pelvis against my sensitive clit. But it's not enough to push me over the edge.

"More," I plead, and Isaac answers with a guttural growl.

He shoves his arms under my knees, raising my legs, while he grabs my hips and starts fucking me fast, deep, and hard. Thank God for my perseverance in years of Pilates, because from this position, he can reach places that human beings shouldn't be able to reach.

He's so deep it almost hurts, but in a pleasurable way. He fucks me with so much intensity I have to cling to his shoulders to not be shoved backwards.

I don't even have time to think when the second orgasm reaches me so suddenly, I bite him on the shoulder through his T-shirt.

I clench around his cock and feel him shudder as he empties himself inside the condom. He strokes a few more times inside me, slow and deep, like he's trying to prolong his pleasure.

We're both breathing hard and he's so spent that he lets my legs down and leans his head on my shoulder. We stay there, embracing and breathing hard for a few long moments before he slips out of me, leaving me empty and trembling.

He pulls back just enough to look at me, his expression softening. "You're something else, Charlotte."

"So are you," I reply, brushing a strand of hair from his face.

For the next few hours, we forget about everything else—our baggage, our fears, the walls we've built around ourselves. We lose ourselves in each other, and the banter and laughter are as much a part of the intimacy as the physical connection.

And when we finally collapse onto the couch, tangled together and completely spent, I can't help but think that maybe trying isn't such a bad idea after all.

10

ISAAC

The hinges on the woodshop door squeak slightly as I push it open, stepping aside to let Charlotte enter first. The scent of sawdust and varnish hangs in the air, familiar and grounding, but today, it feels heavier. Maybe because this is the first time I've let her into this space—*my* space.

Charlotte walks in, her eyes wide as she takes it all in. The workbenches are cluttered with tools and half-finished projects, shelves lined with jars of screws and nails, and in the corner, my prized lathe stands tall and proud.

I try to see it through the eyes of this woman, and all I feel is...simple. She's a *New York Times* best-selling author, used to signing books at big events.

I'm just...me. A guy who makes custom credenzas—a piece of furniture you forget about and is a hassle for your relatives to get rid of once you're dead. I make things that hold value only for the person who buys them; she makes things that are valued by millions. But this is who I am; I appreciate what I have, and I wouldn't change anything about how I make a living.

"This..." she breathes, her voice cracking with awe, "...is incredible."

I didn't realize how much I valued her opinion until I hear it from her lips. The weight lifts from my chest.

"It's just a shop," I say, rubbing the back of my neck. The words sound hollow even to me. I'm not good at receiving compliments, let alone seeing that mesmerized gaze on a woman's face because of what I do.

She spins around to face me, her hands resting on her hips. "Don't you dare downplay this. This isn't just a shop—it's a sanctuary. Look at all of this!"

She gestures to the pieces scattered around—a partially carved headboard, a table with intricate inlays, a chair still waiting for its final coat of polish. Her enthusiasm makes my chest tighten, and I can't tell if it's pride or shame.

"I don't know," I mumble, crossing my arms. "It's just stuff I make."

Is it me, or it's suffocating in here today?

She steps closer, her gaze sharp and unwavering. "Stuff? Are you kidding me? Isaac, this is *art*." There is a bit of scolding in her tone, like she wants me to acknowledge that I'm good at something. Yes, I'm good, but these things come easily to me, so it's not like I make a big deal out of it.

Art. The word feels foreign, almost laughable. I've heard compliments before—a client praising my craftsmanship, a neighbor commenting on my attention to detail—but this is different. This isn't a passing remark; this is *her*. And for some reason, it terrifies me. Why do I care so much about living up to her expectations? She's just a woman who, in a few weeks, will fly back to Chicago, and I won't see her again. And here I am, squirming under her gaze and her words. For some reason, I feel like shit when I think about her leaving.

"You're being dramatic," I mutter, trying to brush it off.

She narrows her eyes. "I am *not* dramatic. Look at this." She points to a low coffee table with a carved edge that mimics the ripple of water. "The detail, the care... Isaac, this is stunning. You should be proud of yourself."

Her words hit me like a punch to the gut. Proud? That's not something I've allowed myself to feel in a long time. And hearing it from her—a woman who writes bestsellers, who knows what it's like to create something that matters—feels too raw, too personal.

I turn away, pretending to inspect the tools on the bench. "It's just a hobby that became a full-time job," I lie, knowing full well it's more than that. When I work on a piece, I enter a state of peace, a world that is mine and only mine. I feel safe there, where nobody can break my heart. The wood won't betray me like a human being can do.

She steps closer, her voice softer now. "You're wrong, you know. This isn't just a hobby. It's a gift."

I clench my jaw, the words sticking in my throat. The last time someone said something about my work, I was holding a ring box, pouring my heart out to someone who didn't want it. And it wasn't a positive comment. What did she say? "I'm not interested in anything you have to offer." That was a blow so low that it gutted me for everyone after her. I haven't even tried to find someone else to spend my life with. The memory stings and I feel the walls going up, the instinct to push her away taking over.

"So," I say, forcing a smug smile on my lips and turning back to her. "Are you going to critique my woodwork, or should we get back to your poses?"

What a lame way to divert the topic. I mean, I really like having sex with her, but it's an abrupt change from the conversation, even for me.

She blinks, clearly thrown off by the sudden shift. "My poses?"

"Yeah," I say, stepping closer, the corner of my mouth twitching up. "You're always testing them out. Maybe it's time we see if one of them works on this furniture."

I see the realization across her face, and I'm happy to discover that there is a pleasant surprise veiled behind it. Luckily, she doesn't think I'm a creep.

Her cheeks flush, and she lets out a nervous laugh. "You're unbelievable, you know that?"

But she bites her lower lip slightly, the same way she always does when she is contemplating the idea of seeing me naked. She's pretty easy to read once you figure out her telltale signs. And right now, she is imagining me between her legs. To be fair, I've imagined her sprawled over that table way too many times to count.

"Maybe." I lean against the workbench, crossing my arms. "But you're curious, aren't you?"

She bites her lip again, with a determined purpose this time, and damn if it doesn't drive me crazy. "Curious about what?"

She pretends to be clueless, but I can see the flicker of lust burning in her eyes. She can't fool me, especially since the air shifted and became charged with the unspoken desire between us. Once I tasted her, once I discovered how she felt coming around my cock, I couldn't get enough of her. She's one of those generous lovers who holds nothing back. When she's into it, she gives you everything. I confess, I didn't expect it, but it was a pleasant surprise.

"Whether or not the poses are as impossible as you think," I point out, even if it's not necessary at all, considering her expression.

Her gaze flicks to the coffee table, then back to me, a mischievous glint in her eye. "You're serious?"

So, she likes that coffee table. I can work with that. To be honest, I've imagined her on every surface in this place. It won't be hard to make her come like I know she wants to. I push off the workbench, closing the distance between us. "You said it yourself—you need to test them. Think of it as... research."

Her laugh is soft, nervous, but there's an unmistakable heat in her eyes now. "You're trouble, Isaac."

"Maybe," I say, my voice low as I reach out to tuck a strand of hair behind her ear. "But you like trouble."

She doesn't argue, and before I can think better of it, I'm kissing her.

The world shrinks to just the two of us—the softness of her lips, the way her hands curl into my shirt, pulling me closer. It's a slow burn, her warmth sinking into me, melting the icy layers I've built around my heart.

When we break apart, we're both breathing hard, and her cheeks are flushed. "Is this going to become a thing with us?" she asks, her voice teasing. "Testing poses?"

"Depends," I say, smirking. "Are they all as interesting as the one on the couch?"

She rolls her eyes but doesn't pull away as I guide her toward the coffee table.

"This one," she says, pointing to the table's edge, "might actually work. Maybe."

"Only one way to find out," I reply, my hands sliding to her waist and turning her around. I put a couple of pieces of cardboards on the floor and make her kneel on them in front of the coffee table. She lets out a nervous giggle, but she doesn't complain when I delicately push her to bend over the wooden surface. She turns around and looks at me over her shoulder.

"Should I take notes?" she asks, smiling mischievously.

"Trust me, I will make sure you won't forget it." I wink at her while I raise the hem of her yellow summer dress over her perfect, round ass. I lower behind her and nip at her butt cheek. She squeals and wriggles at the attention. I tease her clit over her panties, and she moans.

"Do you want me to repeat that? To be sure you remember it." My voice comes out hoarse and strained by the effort not to fuck her brains out here and now. I want to enjoy every second of it.

"Yes!" she groans. "I definitely need a repeat. I didn't..." She can't finish the sentence because another throaty moan escapes her lips.

"Like that?" I whisper, bending down to reach her ear.

She breathes hard and closes her eyes. "You are going to kill me." She lets out a whimper while I push my erection against her ass.

"Sweetheart, I haven't even started," I grumble against her back while I kiss my way down from her neck to the base of her spine. When I reach her panty-covered butt, I grab the fabric and slowly pull it down her fit legs. She wriggles to help me remove them when I reach her knees, and I throw them to the side.

I sit on my heels and start to unbutton my pants while I admire the work of art that is her butt. It's round and perfect, and that pink slit is already wet and ready for me. She is there at my complete mercy, and I can't wait to slip into her and get lost in her moans and sweet whimpers.

I free my cock, and roll up a condom that I fish from my back pocket, then grab her right leg and raise her knee over the coffee table.

She looks back over her shoulder with a mischievous smile on her face. "I like it when you experiment with my book," she purrs.

Seeing her so open and ready for me makes me almost come on the spot. "Happy to help. I deserve a sentence or two in your acknowledgments." I wink at her.

She giggles. "A dedication. I swear you deserve a dedication and nothing less."

I align my erection to her opening and push all

the way in without encountering any resistance. We both quit talking, lost in the pleasure of this moment. She closes her eyes, grabs the edge of the coffee table, and pushes her butt back against my hips.

It's heaven.

I slowly pull back and thrust into her again, enjoying how tight she is around my shaft. She couldn't be more perfect. I'll never find anyone like her ever again, and the thought tugs some unpleasant feeling at the bottom of my heart I refuse to acknowledge. She's here now. We're enjoying each other, and it's enough for now.

"More, please," she moans, and a smug smile curves my lips.

"As you wish," I say while thrusting into her like our lives depend on it.

She groans and arches her back, grabbing the edge of the coffee table even tighter. I take it as a request to thrust harder, and I do it. The coffee table screeches under my assault and slips forward. I grip one hand next to Charlotte's white knuckles, trying to stop it, but with little success.

But I can't stop now. Not when she is panting and wriggling her ass, and I'm reaching the peak of my pleasure. She comes with a loud moan and clenches around my cock, sending me over the edge and milking my orgasm. Wave after wave of pure pleasure runs under my skin, reaching every part of my body.

I lower myself over her back, trying to regain my breath and, at the same time, trying not to crush her with my weight.

She lets out a breathless laugh, and I follow with my own chuckle.

"Okay, the coffee table is for sweet lovemaking. Got it." She giggles.

"We could try the credenza next time," I suggest.

She nods. "Give me some time to recover. I can't feel my legs," she says, lowering her knee from where I'd put it.

I wrap her in my arms and let her sit in my lap to avoid her having to sit on the cold concrete. I hold her there, and for a long moment, I enjoy her warmth against my chest. It's just us—no past memories, no fears, just the thrill of being together.

As I lower my face into her hair and inhale her scent deeply, I look around this place with new eyes. I can't help but wonder if maybe she's right. Perhaps this is art—what I've created. And for the first time in years, I let myself feel proud.

11

CHARLOTTE

The sunlight filters through the curtains of my rental, painting the walls with streaks of red and orange. I sit cross-legged on the couch, my laptop balanced on my knees. At least the smell of garlic and onions is gone, and no raccoons, either. I call it a victory. I spent so much time in Isaac's home that I almost forgot I rented this place to write my book. It feels like it was a lifetime ago, but it's barely been over a month and a half.

So much has changed in this time period. *I've* changed.

Staring at the lawyer's contact on my phone, my heart feels heavy, and my thumb seems paralyzed over the call button.

Just do it, Charlotte.

I take a deep breath, hit *Call,* and press the phone to my ear.

"Charlotte," James, my lawyer, greets me after a couple of rings. "Good morning. I wasn't expecting to hear from you. Do we have an appointment that I forgot?" His doubt creeps through the phone.

"Morning, James. No, I'm not calling for that." My voice is shaky, and I clear my throat. "I've made a decision about the house," I blurt out all in one breath.

There's a brief pause during which I don't even know if he is breathing. My ex and I have gone back and forth so many times without coming to any agreement that I think James lost hope of finding a solution that didn't involve a judge splitting the property.

Then I hear a cautious, "Alright. What's the plan?"

I stare at the patch of carpet in front of me, threading my fingers through my hair. "I'll sell it. You can let Mark know that I agree to his terms."

The long moment of silence makes me doubt my decision. Maybe he thinks I'm doing the wrong thing, but something in me has changed, and I'm ready to let my past go. If this means giving in to my ex-husband's demands, so be it. It's just a house.

"Are you sure?" James's voice softens. "I know this hasn't been an easy choice for you."

"It hasn't," I admit, exhaling slowly. "But I've realized something. I've been clinging to that house, not because I need it, but because of what it represents. The memories, the moments we shared...they're tied to that place, but they're not in the walls or the furniture. They're in me."

I can always carry the good memories with me without the reminder of the bad ones when I walk into those rooms.

There's a long exhale, and then James asks, "And you're okay with letting it go?"

I know he's asking because I was so adamant about needing my office to keep writing that he wants to be sure I'm okay with whatever the future holds for me. I cried so much in his office over that damn house, I can understand why he's confused.

"Yes." I nod, even though he can't see me. "Mark can't take my memories. He can do whatever he wants with the house—the physical structure—but the life I built there—*my* life—doesn't depend on bricks and mortar. He wants to sell it and split the money? So be it." My voice comes out more convincing this time.

The more I repeat it out loud, the better I feel.

That heavy weight on my chest is becoming lighter and lighter as the reality of my decision sinks in. Why did I wait so long to do this? The answer comes to my mind in the form of a grumpy bearded man. Meeting Isaac made me realize that I have an entire life to live, and I can't cling to the past, wasting my present and my future.

"You're stronger than most people, Charlotte," he says with a note of admiration in his tone.

I laugh softly. "I don't know about that. I just know I'm ready to move on. The house isn't my home anymore, and it hasn't been for a long time. It's time to start fresh."

"Understood. I'll handle the paperwork and contact Mark's lawyer. I'll keep you updated on the process." I can hear the smile in his voice, as if he's finally been given the solution he's been waiting for.

He's a good man. He always advised me on the best decisions I could make in this situation, but he never pressured me to do something I wasn't convinced was right for me. He never pressured me to speed up my divorce just so he could get paid and consider the job done. He listened to me and gave me all the time I needed to process what was happening.

"Thank you, James. Really."

"Anytime. And Charlotte?" His voice is kind.

"Yeah?"

"I hope this decision brings you the peace you deserve."

There is such genuine care in his words that they settle over me like a comforting blanket. "I hope so too."

We end the call, and I set the phone down on the coffee table, staring at it like it can change my life. And it actually just did. That phone call opened so many possibilities, my heart is hammering in my chest with excitement, anticipation, and a bit of fear.

I always thought I would lose a part of me with that house, but I realize I just gained my freedom.

A knock echoes through the space before I can get too lost in my thoughts. Frowning, I glance at the door. It's not like I know a ton of people in this place.

When I open it, Isaac is standing there, his hands shoved into the pockets of his jeans, his face a mix of worry and embarrassment. His broad frame fills the doorway, and for a moment, I'm caught off guard.

"What are you doing here?" I ask, gripping the handle and not moving an inch.

I'm not used to having him here. Heck, *I* am not used to being here. I'm so taken aback by his visit that I'm frozen in place. At this moment, it hits me what a weird relationship we have. I'm comfortable coming and going from his house like it's my home, but I feel strange when he knocks at my door. Talk about unusual choices I've made in the past couple of months.

He gives me a once-over, furrowing his brow. "You weren't at the house today. I thought something happened." His voice is uncertain, as if he thinks he has overstepped coming here.

I blink, touched by his concern. "I just needed to stay here for the day. I had a call to make."

He steps inside without waiting for an invitation, his presence instantly making the room feel smaller. "Is everything okay? You look flustered."

I haven't had the chance to look at myself in the mirror, but I imagine I appear a bit disheveled, considering how many times I've run my hands through my hair and fidgeted with the hem of my tank top.

"I called my lawyer," I say, closing the door behind him.

His eyes narrow slightly, but he doesn't say anything, waiting for me to continue.

"I told him I'd sell the house," I explain, crossing my arms over my chest.

I've explained to him over time why I ended up

here in Pinecreek. He knows everything about my asshole husband.

Isaac's expression softens, and he tilts his head. "That's...a big decision. You okay?"

I nod, though my throat feels tight. "I am. I realized I was holding onto the house because I thought letting it go meant losing everything I'd built. But that's not true. The memories are mine, no matter where I live. And, honestly, I don't want anything tying me to my past anymore."

He studies me for a long moment, then asks, "So, where will you go?"

I shrug, letting out a breathy laugh. "I have no idea. Somewhere new, I guess. Somewhere that doesn't come with baggage."

I honestly didn't think about it. It hadn't even crossed my mind until Isaac brought it up. I was so eager to be done with all of it that I didn't give a thought to the future—something I've never done in my entire life. I'm the queen of plans and schedules.

His lips quirk up in a small, almost imperceptible smile. "That's brave."

"Or reckless," I counter, grinning.

"Maybe both."

There's a pause, and I realize how close we're standing. The air between us feels charged, the kind of tension that makes it hard to breathe. His dark eyes search mine, and I can't tell if he's trying to figure me out or if he's just trying to keep his own thoughts in check.

Since when did we become awkward with each other? We've had sex on every surface of his house, for Pete's sake. But that was in the bubble of his house. Here, the world keeps spinning around us, and the reality is a heavy burden between us. His question about the future has put an expiration date on what we had, and I'm not sure how I feel about it. The disappointment creeps into my chest, along with the feeling that this is going too fast and ending too soon, but I don't know how to stop it.

"Well," he says, finally, stepping back. "I guess I'll leave you to it. Just...don't disappear on me without a heads-up again, okay?"

I smile, touched by his words even though he delivers them in his usual gruff tone. "I'll try not to."

He gives a short nod, then turns to leave, but not before glancing back at me. "If you need anything, you know where to find me."

That sentence sounds like it has a deeper meaning, like he wouldn't mind being part of my complicated baggage. So, where does this leave us? I don't know if I have the energy to have that conversation right now. The decision I made this morning drained me to the point that I can barely focus on his presence here.

"I do," I say softly, watching as he disappears out the door.

As it closes behind him, I feel a strange mix of emotions—gratitude, relief, and something else I can't put my finger on.

One thing is certain: letting go of the past feels less daunting with someone like Isaac nearby.

12

ISAAC

Charlotte lies next to me, her body warm against mine, her soft laughter vibrating through the quiet room. The sheets are tangled around her waist, and her hair spills over my pillow like a messy halo. Her skin is flushed, her lips swollen from our last round of whatever the hell we're doing here.

After I went to her house yesterday like a lovesick puppy, she came back late in the afternoon with her laptop tucked under her arm and a lightness in her smile that wasn't there before. It's like she's left behind the burden of her past and started a new life.

I admire her for that. I still feel pulled by mine like a ball and chain I can't get rid of. But when she came into my living room, I felt a surge of excitement running from my stomach to every part of my body.

She makes my days better.

"Stop grinning like that," she says, swatting my chest lightly.

"Like what?" I ask, knowing exactly what she means.

"Like you just won the lottery."

I chuckle, pulling her closer. "Well, if the prize involves you naked in my bed, I think I did."

I don't think I'll ever get enough of her body, her moans, her hands on me, her pussy clenching around my cock. She's perfect on so many levels I just can't get enough of *her*.

She groans, burying her face in her hands. "Why do you have to be so smug?"

"It's one of my best qualities," I tease.

"Debatable."

I grab her wrists gently, tugging her hands away from her face so I can see her expression. Her eyes are shining, her smile impossible to contain. It's a look I'm starting to crave, even though I know better. This happiness is coming to an end. When her book is done, she'll disappear from this place, and only the memories of her will be left in this house.

"So, what's the plan now?" I ask, trying to sound casual. "Another chapter to write?"

I realize I'm counting the days left for her to be here. And it's kind of daunting. She slipped into my heart without me realizing it, and now I'm scared to lose her.

She surprises me by shaking her head. "Nope. It's done."

My heart sinks. What does she mean? This is the end of our journey?

I blink, thrown off balance. "What's done?" I ask, knowing full well that I clearly understand what she means.

"The book."

I stare at her, processing her words. "You finished it? Like, completely?" Shouldn't there be some revisions to do? It can't just be finished.

"Completely," she says, her voice brimming with pride. "Last night was the final sprint. I'm done."

She says it like a burden was lifted from her shoulders, and it's probably exactly like that. When I finish one of my pieces, I'm overwhelmed by a mixture of feelings, from disbelief to relief, and also satisfaction. They are so conflicting that it takes me a couple of days to calm down the turmoil inside and start a new piece.

"Wow," I say, meaning it. "That's...incredible." And it really is. I have always admired her for being able to write an entire book. It amazes me how effortless she makes it seem when I know it's far from it. An entire book! I can't even focus long enough to write a grocery list.

"It feels surreal," she admits, her smile softening. "Every time I finish a book, it's like crossing the finish line of a marathon—exhausting but exhilarating."

I know the feeling. After you finish something so massive, you just want to crawl into bed and not touch one of your tools again—until you feel the urge to immerse yourself in a new project again. You will always crave another one.

I brush a strand of hair from her cheek, fighting the urge to kiss her again. "So, what now? Write another one?"

I'm not ready to let her go. Another book is reasonable, right? A series! They write series now. She should think about it. A long series of books inspired by this house sounds reasonable to me. Anything but this feeling of her slipping between my fingers.

She grins wickedly. "Or stop having sex. You're very distracting."

Well, *that* will never happen. After tasting her, she'll have to hit me with a bat to make me give up that part of our relationship.

I smirk, trailing my fingers lazily down her arm. "Good luck with that."

"Cocky," she mutters, but there's no bite in her words.

"Confident," I correct, earning an eye roll.

Her laughter fades, and I catch a flicker of something in her expression—an emotion I can't quite name but recognize all the same. She's thinking about what comes next, and suddenly, I feel like I'm standing on the edge of a cliff. What if she doesn't consider me in her future? I mean, she is like a tourist here, it's not like she's going to give up her life somewhere else to stay here with me. As much as I want that, it's not realistic. So what? We just part ways like this never happened? For the first time since my ex, I've found the will to open up to someone else, and losing her is going to hurt. A lot.

"Where will you go now?" I ask, trying to keep my tone even. My chest is another story. I don't think I've ever been so overwhelmed by anxiety as in this moment.

She sighs, tracing patterns on my chest with her fingertips. "I still have a couple of weeks left on the rental I barely used. After that...I don't know yet. Somewhere new, I think. I have to start from scratch when it comes to my personal life, and I honestly don't know where to start."

Her words hit me harder than I expected. I should be happy for her—proud, even. She's ready to move on, to start fresh. But all I can think about is how empty my house is going to feel without her in it.

"Sounds exciting," I say, forcing a smile. "You have the whole world to explore."

"I do," she agrees, her voice soft.

There's a pause, the kind that feels heavier than it should. I want to tell her to stay, but the words catch in my throat. She doesn't owe me anything, and I've got no right to ask her for more than she's willing to give. She's a famous author going on tours, doing interviews, and going to conferences. Yes, I looked her up, and I regret it. It reminded me that I have nothing to offer her. I can't put anything on the table.

"Can I read it?" I ask instead, nodding toward her laptop on the nightstand.

Her eyes widen, and she shakes her head vehemently. "Absolutely not."

She almost squeals, and I laugh at her panicked

expression. It's as if I asked her to erase the manuscript from her computer.

"Why not?

"Because it's not polished yet," she says, sitting up and wrapping the sheet around her like a makeshift toga. "No one reads my first drafts. Not even my editor. It's my rule."

Go figure. Isn't the editor supposed to do exactly that? Read the book and polish it.

I raise an eyebrow. "Not even me?"

"Especially not you."

Well, that sucks. It's not like I ever read romances, but this one was created in my living room. I'm curious about it. Especially because I helped with the research. And we did that a lot.

Her determination makes me grin. "I'm not going to judge it. I just want to see what all the fuss is about. I contributed to that book, you know?" I wave my hand between my naked body and hers.

"No," she says firmly, crossing her arms. "Not happening."

She is pouting now. She didn't even laugh at my reference to "the poses." She really doesn't want me to read it.

"Alright, alright," I say, holding up my hands in surrender. "I won't push."

But I can't deny that I'm curious. She's poured herself into that book for weeks, and I want to know what's inside her head—the worlds she creates, the characters she brings to life. It's not just about the book. It's about *her*.

She relaxes, dropping her guard, and I take the opportunity to pull her back down beside me. She resists for about half a second before giving in, her body fitting against mine like she belongs here.

"You're insufferable," she mumbles, her voice muffled against my chest.

"And yet, here you are," I tease, wrapping an arm around her waist.

Her laughter vibrates against me, and for a moment, everything feels right. But in the back of my mind, the clock is ticking, counting down the days until she's gone.

I don't know what's worse—the thought of her leaving or the fact that I'm already dreading it.

13

CHARLOTTE

I push open the door to Isaac's house, already forming the words to demand why he didn't meet me for coffee as we had planned yesterday. It was the first time we've decided to go out for breakfast. Last night, I decided to go to my rental to catch up on a long list of emails that I couldn't put off anymore. If I'd stayed here, I would have ended up in his bed and got nothing done.

He grumbled his disappointment, undressed me, fucked me thoroughly one last time, and agreed to come to pick me up half an hour ago. But this morning, he didn't show up. So, here I am, trying to figure out what happened in the last few hours we've been separated.

"Isaac?" I call from across the kitchen as I put my bag on the counter.

I stop in my tracks when I spot him sitting on the couch, his hair disheveled, eyes bloodshot, holding something in his hands.

My manuscript.

I accidentally left the printed copy here. When I couldn't find it last night, I assumed I had forgotten it, but I also assumed it was safe when I told him not to read it. Well, clearly, I was mistaken.

He looks up as my shoes click on the wood floor; his expression is unreadable, and my stomach clenches in an unpleasant grip.

"Isaac?" I ask cautiously, even though I know exactly what's going on.

How could he betray my trust like that? I explicitly told him I wasn't comfortable with him reading it before it was ready. I thought he had listened to me. I thought he *respected* me.

"You didn't tell me you left a copy of your book here," he says, his voice low and tight.

Why do I feel like he's accusing me of something? Is he for real now? *He* is reading something I asked him not to. Why is he trying to make me feel guilty?

"I...didn't think I needed to," I say, my defenses rising. "It's not like I expected you to *read* it."

He scoffs, setting the stack of papers on the coffee table with an air of finality. "You didn't think I'd be curious? You wrote it while staying in my house, Charlotte. Half the time, you wouldn't shut up about it."

I may have mentioned something here and there—okay, more than something—but those were ideas, plot twists, and my brainstorming. I was comfortable sharing that with him. This is a whole other level of trust, and he betrayed it.

My cheeks flush hot. "That doesn't give you the right to invade my privacy!"

"Privacy?" he snaps, standing abruptly. "You left it lying here! What did you expect? For me to pretend it wasn't there?"

Is he trying to blame me? If he thinks I will apologize for that, he has a long wait ahead of him. I have never felt so exposed and violated in my entire life. Writing a book is something personal, something I pour my heart into. It's a living thing I nurture from inception until its publication. It's something I cherish and enjoy for myself, until I publish it and it becomes something that's not mine anymore, but my readers'. It's for every single person who reads it and resonates with it. He barged, unin-vited, into a corner of my life that is mine alone.

"Yes!" I shout back. "That's exactly what I expected because I trusted you!"

His expression darkens, and he grips the bunch of papers so tightly his knuckles turn white. He is clearly furious, and I'm a bit taken aback because I'm the one who should be mad. Not him. He got caught doing something he shouldn't have and he should deal with the consequences. This is not how I expected him to react. Did I misjudge him that badly, or am I missing something?

His eyes narrow, and the tension in the room thickens. "And I trusted you not to turn *us* into a goddamn sideshow for your readers."

Well, this is definitely not what I expected him to say. I'm so baffled my brain can't formulate a coherent response to his accusation.

I blink, stunned. "What are you talking about?"

He points to the manuscript like it's a loaded weapon. "Don't play dumb, Charlotte. The details. The scenes. The *poses*. You wrote about *us*."

Is he serious right now? We've been joking about the poses this whole time, saying it was research, and now he's complaining about it? Apparently, I should've had him sign a contract for permission to include his "trademarked shenanigans." I may write about them, but I will never understand men!

"That's not—" I start, but he cuts me off.

"Don't deny it," he growls, stepping closer. "You think I wouldn't recognize it? The things we said? The way you described everything in such detail, down to the scar on my shoulder?"

Well, I can remove that if he's worried about someone recognizing him. Clearly, no one else in the world has a scar on their shoulder. Eight billion people, and he's the only one. Asshole.

"It's sex, Isaac!" I snap, my voice rising to match his. "Everybody does it like that. It's not just about *you*. Do you really think no one else ever thought to fuck on a coffee table?"

He is unbelievable. He was all peacocking around like a caveman, "I'll show you how it's done," and then he chickens out when I actually wrote about it.

His jaw clenches, and for a moment, I think he might explode. Instead, his voice drops, cold and dripping venom. "That's exactly what my ex used to say. 'It's not about you, Isaac.' Turns out, I was just a convenient tool for whatever she needed. And now, here you are, using me for *material*."

The words hit me like a slap to the face. My chest

tightens, anger and hurt colliding in a messy tangle. He thinks I'm like his ex? Jesus, how did things get so bad that he can't even see this situation is different? I literally told him I was doing research for my book; it's not like I hid something from him.

"How dare you," I whisper, my voice trembling.

I'm so angry right now. I feel the tears pushing to get out, but I won't give him the satisfaction of seeing me cry. He doesn't deserve my sadness, let alone my tears.

"How dare *I*?" he fires back. "You turned something private—something *real*—into garbage for your book, and you expect me to be okay with it?"

Wow. This is a new level of cruelty. I may not be writing high literature, but telling me it's garbage is a new low. I'm used to being considered a "lesser author" for the genre I write, and in the beginning, I cried about it, but now I brush it off. But hearing it from him hurts. A lot.

"Do you even hear yourself right now?" I snap. "You're accusing me of being like your ex because I wrote a sex scene? You think I don't care about you? About *this*?" I gesture wildly between us, my heart pounding.

I don't know if he thinks I sleep with just anyone willing to give me something to write about, but if so, he knows nothing about me. And this hurts even more because I thought we had something.

Isaac's eyes soften for a fraction of a second, but then his defenses slam back into place. "You tell me, Charlotte. Was it just research for you? Another chapter to finish?"

My hands curl into fists, my nails digging into my palms. "I can't believe you'd even think that. After everything...after *us*."

The anger boiling in my stomach makes my mouth taste sour. The bile rising in my throat threatens to spill onto the floor.

"Then explain it to me," he demands, his voice rough. "Explain how you can write about something so personal and not even think to ask how I'd feel about it."

I stare at him, the weight of his accusation pressing down on me like a boulder. He doesn't trust me. He doesn't see me as anything more than another person out to hurt him. I haven't written about him, I wrote about how he makes me feel about him, how my body responds to him. How we are so connected, it's like we are one soul sharing two bodies. When we are entangled between the sheets, that separation is so thin we could easily be one person.

"You know what?" I say, and my voice is icy. "I don't owe you an explanation. Not when you've already made up your mind about who I am."

I grab my things, including the damn manuscript from his hands, and I scramble to get out of this house as soon as possible.

"Charlotte—" He tries to grab my wrist, but I wriggle out of his grasp.

"No," I cut him off, grabbing my bag from where I dropped it on the counter. "You don't get to paint me as the villain in your sad little narrative, Isaac. I'm not your ex, and I'm not here to use you."

He opens his mouth to respond, but I don't give him the chance. I turn my back and stalk to the door, stopping right before turning the handle.

"Enjoy the rest of your life being miserable and alone," I snap, my voice cracking. "Because, clearly, that's what you want."

I slam the door behind me, my heart shattering with every step I take away from his house.

14

ISAAC

I didn't sleep. Not really. I spent most of the night staring at the ceiling, replaying the fight with Charlotte over and over in my head. Her words, sharp and furious, cut deeper than I want to admit.

And mine feel rough in my throat. I shouldn't have said what I did. Especially the part about her books being garbage. Jesus, the hurt in her eyes was so raw it bled. How could I have been so cruel? That wasn't me talking, it was my anger and my fear.

This morning, the house feels too quiet. Too empty. Her absence is a physical thing, like a gaping wound I can't ignore. I shove my boots on and head out, not really knowing where I'm going until I'm halfway to Henry's store. But I can't spend a single minute inside that place that smells like her and reminds me how much of an asshole I've been.

When I step inside, the bell jingles and the smell of freshly baked bread and ground coffee greets me. Henry is behind the counter, stacking boxes of crackers like it's the most important job in the world. He always says he's tired and wants to sell this place, but I don't think he'd last one day without being here chatting with his customers and making them feel at home.

He looks up and grins. "Well, well. If it isn't our town hermit gracing us with his presence."

I don't have the strength to fight about what he calls me, so I manage a weak smile and rub the back of my neck. "Morning, Henry."

He studies me for a moment, his cheerful expression dimming. "You look like hell, son. Trouble sleeping?"

Of course, he noticed. He's like a father to all of us. He worries about each person in this small town and he lets you know about it. In the most fatherly, and sometimes thankless, way.

"You could say that." My voice comes out rough from my lack of rest and coffee. I had to run out to the house before my brain caught up with the fact that Charlotte wasn't there making coffee for both of us this morning. A lot of good that did, considering I'm here thinking exactly that.

He sets down the box and leans on the counter, his sharp eyes boring into mine. "Let me guess. This has something to do with that pretty writer lady who's been hanging around?"

I hesitate, then nod. Henry's been here longer than anyone, and while he might not be the kind of guy to hand out hugs and pats on the back, he's seen his share of people and problems. If anyone can help me make sense of this mess, it's him. Funny how I never wanted to share my life with him, but now he's the only person who I'm sure won't judge me for my mistakes.

"Got time to talk?" I ask, my voice low.

If he's surprised by my request, he doesn't show it, but I'm not shocked. He gossips a lot, but not about deeply personal things; for that, he knows how to keep a secret. And he's wise enough to know when to keep things to himself. He also has the patience to listen to people who need to talk. And I definitely need to do that now.

He gestures to the small café corner of the store. "Always."

We sit down on the worn wooden stools facing the counter with the coffee machine, and Henry pours us each a cup from the pot behind the counter.

"So," he starts, folding his hands on the counter-top. "What's eating you?" Straight to the point.

I take a sip of the coffee, stalling. It's bitter and strong, just the way I like it. Finally, I set the cup down and look him in the eye.

"I messed up, Henry." There is no other way to put it. I royally fucked up, and I don't know how to fix this mess.

His eyebrows lift slightly, but he doesn't say anything, just waits for me to continue.

"I...read something I shouldn't have," I admit, my stomach twisting with guilt.

The truth is, I was angry with her mostly because she caught me doing something I shouldn't have done. I was so deep in my thoughts, recognizing myself and my emotions all over the pages, that when she caught me, I snapped and got defensive.

He nods slowly. "Go on."

"It was her manuscript," I say, the words tumbling out. "The one she's been working on while staying here. She left a copy at my house, and I... I got curious." That is an understatement. I considered the fact that I shouldn't have started reading it halfway through the book. But that didn't stop me. I just went straight to the last page.

Henry leans back in his stool, his expression unreadable. "And?"

"And it...it pissed me off," I confess, the frustration bubbling up again. "I saw parts of me in it—the grumpy guy, you know? But it could've been anyone. I didn't recognize *me*. Not exactly."

I recognized my feelings. She could read me so well that I saw my soul on display on those pages, and I freaked out. Nobody's ever seen me like that. She really *saw* me. And it's terrifying.

Henry tilts his head, considering. "So, you're mad because you think she used you as a model for one of her characters?"

"Yes—no. I don't know," I groan, running a hand through my hair. "The grumpy guy...yeah, okay, that's me. But that's not what got under my skin."

He raises an eyebrow, waiting for me to elaborate. I know he's on pins and needles, wanting to know more, but he restrains himself from pushing, probably for fear I might close up completely. But my hurt feels too raw and open to stop sharing about it now.

"It was the...intimate stuff," I admit, heat creeping up my neck. "The things we've done together, the things we've shared...she put it in the book, Henry. It felt...personal."

Now, this is something I never imagined talking about, let alone with Henry. I never talk about my sex life, not even with my friends at school, mostly because there wasn't much action back in the day. But also, because I'm a pretty private guy, I guess.

Henry strokes his chin thoughtfully. "And you told her that?"

"I confronted her, yeah," I say, shifting uncomfortably. "But she said it's just sex, that everyone does it like that. Like it wasn't special."

That's where everything went wrong. I was so angry for exposing my real self to her, and her treating it like it was nothing, that I said a bunch of stuff I shouldn't have said. Like comparing her to my ex. What the heck was I thinking?

Henry's lips twitch like he's trying not to smile. "And that got to you, didn't it?" His eyes light up like he's hit the jackpot. Damn Henry and his habit of sticking his nose into other people's business. And damn me for giving him exactly what he wants.

"Damn right, it did," I snap. "Because it *is* special. At least, it is to me."

He leans forward, his eyes piercing me and making me squirm on my stool. "So, what's the real problem here, Isaac? Is it that she wrote about it, or is it that you care more than you're willing to admit?"

I sit back, the question hitting me like a punch in the gut. Reading that book brought to the surface the reality that she would disappear from my life, and I could do nothing to stop it. I wasn't ready to let her go, especially after that book showed me what I could have had with her, and it was slipping from my fingers so fast I couldn't process it. I panicked. And then I made it worse.

Henry continues, his voice steady. "You said you didn't recognize yourself in the book, right? But maybe that's because you're looking at it wrong. She's a writer, Isaac. She takes pieces of life—of people—and turns them into stories. It's not a mirror; it's a mosaic."

When did he get so wise? Maybe I should listen to him more. I let his words sink in momentarily, staring into my coffee. "So, you're saying I over-reacted?"

"I'm saying you need to figure out why it upset you so much," he says. "You're not mad because she wrote a book. You're mad because it feels like she took something private and shared it with the world. And that only bothers you because it matters to you."

His words hit harder than I'd like to admit. He's right. I wouldn't care so much if it didn't mean something. I was so caught up in my feelings that I barked out my frustrations instead of counting to ten and thinking twice before voicing them.

"I didn't want to admit it," I say quietly. "Not even to myself."

Henry nods, a small smile playing on his lips. "Well, there you go. Now, the question is, what are you going to do about it?"

I shake my head. "I don't know. She's furious with me. She left, slamming the door. She might not forgive me."

Henry chuckles, the sound warm and reassuring. "Oh, she'll be back. That woman's got fire, but she's not the type to walk away without a fight. The real question is, are you ready to fight for her?"

What if she doesn't want me to fight for her? You can only fight for someone if they still feel something for you. But what if my words killed any kind of feeling she may have for me? She's got an asshole for an ex. Maybe she doesn't want another one that puts up an angry wall the first time he feels vulnerable. We're not kids anymore. I'm sure she wants an emotionally stable guy, not a child to raise.

But there's no way to tell my heart all of this

because its stubborn beat picks up speed just thinking about her. Who's going to explain to it that everything might already be lost?

I don't answer right away. Instead, I let Henry's words sink in, the truth of them settling deep in my chest.

"Thanks, Henry," I say finally, standing and reaching for my wallet.

He waves me off. "Don't thank me yet. You've still got work to do."

I nod, the weight of his words heavy but oddly comforting. As I leave the store, I feel a glimmer of something I haven't felt in a long time. Something my heart clings hard to.

Hope.

15

CHARLOTTE

Christine sips her latte, her keen eyes skimming over me as we sit in our favorite corner of The Beanery. The coffee shop is bustling, but I barely notice the noise. My chest feels tight, and the world outside my mind is muffled, like I'm underwater.

I gave her the manuscript right before I packed my things and left, and when I landed in Chicago, she had already read it. She picked me up at the airport and brought me here before going to my apartment. I don't know if I did the right thing coming here because, right now, I just want to cry, crawl under a thick blanket, and wake up knowing this was only a bad dream.

"Charlotte," Christine says, her tone sharp

enough to cut through the fog in my head. "You're not even listening to me."

I can't even hear my thoughts, let alone her voice. "Sorry," I murmur, stirring my coffee for the fifth time without taking a sip.

Christine narrows her eyes. "You're acting strange. Usually, you're bouncing off the walls after turning in a manuscript. What's going on?"

I'm not surprised she noticed my mood. It doesn't take a genius to understand that I'm far from fine. Even the flight attendant gave me two glasses of wine without me asking. I feel *that* bad.

I bite my lip and glance at the stack of papers on the table between us. My manuscript. *The* manuscript. The one I poured my heart and soul into, only to have it tear me apart. This is the first time a book feels so personal that I can't separate it from reality. When I started in this career, the first rule I gave myself was to always let the manuscript go. Let it live its own life without me cradling it. This time it's different.

She picks up the stack and flips through it, her red-painted nails in stark contrast against the white pages. "Let me tell you this much, Charlotte. This is the best thing you've ever written."

Her voice is soft but firm. I never considered this

book any better than the others. But that's nothing new. I can't be the judge of something I wrote myself, especially so soon after writing "The End" on the final page.

I look up sharply. "You think so?"

Her smile softens her features. She puts a hand on my bouncing leg and squeezes reassuringly.

"Not think, darling. Know," Christine says, setting the pages down with a firm thud. "It's raw, it's heartfelt, it's sexy as hell. This book has bestseller written all over it."

Her words should fill me with pride, maybe even relief. Instead, my stomach twists. I should be happy, but the only thing I feel is dread that I'm making a huge mistake. I can't shake the feeling that something's not right about those pages.

"You don't look happy," she says, frowning. "This is the part where you usually do that awkward little victory dance of yours."

I know. But I don't feel anything close to victory this time. On the contrary, I feel like the biggest loser. I manage a weak smile. "I'm glad you like it. Really."

Christine leans forward, concern etched into her usually unflappable face. "Charlotte, talk to me. You look more miserable now than you did during your divorce. And let me remind you, that was a pretty low bar."

I flinch at her bluntness but don't deny it. She's right. I feel worse now than I ever did after signing those divorce papers.

"I told my lawyer to sell the house." I don't know why I tell her this, because it has nothing to do with how I feel, but it's a start.

She raises her eyebrows, surprised. "And how do you feel about that? I know that's a big deal for you." She's cautious, and I understand why. This topic has triggered way too many rants on my end about my asshole ex.

"Honestly? I feel relieved. I should have done it sooner." I smile at her, then lower my gaze to the coffee when it miserably falters.

"So, it's not the book or the house. What is bothering you? You're worrying me." Her tone has so much concern that I look back at her.

"I think I messed up, Christine," I say softly.

She arches a perfectly shaped brow. "Messed up, how? From what I can see, you've just delivered a masterpiece, and you got rid of that burden of a house. Do you regret it? You just said you're relieved."

I understand her confusion. My head feels the

same right now. A massive tangle of thoughts and feelings.

I shake my head, my hands tightening around the coffee cup. "It's not about the writing or the house. It's about Isaac."

"The hot woodworker you've been shacking up with?" she asks, smirking.

I'm starting to regret telling her about that during one of our phone calls. I reassured her I was writing and not hiding away in a foreign country. I never went into detail, but I might have slipped in the fact that we had dinner together.

"We haven't been—" I stop, sighing. "Okay, fine. Yes, him."

Christine's smirk fades. "What about him?"

I swallow hard, the guilt pressing down on me like a heavy weight. "The book...it's about him. Or at least, parts of it are. The intimate scenes, the way the male lead acts...those were all inspired by him."

Her eyes widen. "Oh."

"Yeah. *Oh.*"

"It was *that* good?" She sounds almost envious.

I let out a nervous chuckle. "Yes, but that's not the point."

Christine sits back, crossing her arms. "So, what's the problem? Did he find out?"

I nod, feeling a lump rise in my throat. "He read it. Without asking, by the way, but that's beside the point. The point is, he was furious. He said I betrayed his trust."

And this thought is nagging me to the point that I want to throw up. I didn't mean to use him as the main character of my story, at least, not intentionally, but everything about him is so good he might as well be written by a woman, and he ended up in those pages. Not him as a person, but him as a feeling. How he makes *me* feel. How I felt complete and free and vulnerable in the best way possible. He made me *feel*, and those feelings powered my writing like nothing before.

Christine's lips purse, and she nods slowly. "I can see how he might feel that way. Isaac doesn't exactly strike me as the type who wants his private life splashed across the pages of a book. I mean, if the book is any indication of what he's like."

"There's no way anyone could identify him," I protest, trying to convince myself more than her— she didn't recognize him until I brought it up. "No names, no references to Pinecreek or his woodshop. But the intimate stuff...he knew. He was there; he lived those moments. And now I realize how deeply personal it was to him."

Christine studies me for a moment, then leans forward. "Charlotte, are you in love with him?"

The question hits me like a lightning bolt. I open my mouth to respond, but the words catch in my throat. I can deny it until I die, but it doesn't change the reality.

"Charlotte."

"Yes," I whisper, tears stinging my eyes. "I love him. And I ruined everything."

The reality sinks in like concrete pouring into my chest. Making it difficult to breathe.

Christine reaches across the table and grabs my hand. "Sweetheart, you didn't ruin anything. You made a mistake. It happens. The real question is, what are you going to do about it?"

I shake my head, tears slipping down my cheeks. "He'll never forgive me. I invaded his privacy. I turned something sacred into...into material for my book. I didn't even ask him or explain what I was doing. I just assumed he'd never know, never care."

I assumed when we did "research," he knew I would use those things, or at least part of them, in a romanticized way, but it never occurred to me that it was more than something shallow for him. All those references he made to my book were a way to connect with me on a deeper level than I was even aware of. He brought me to his sanctuary, we made love there, and I used it to fill the pages of my book.

"But he did care," Christine says gently. "And that's telling, isn't it?"

It's downright screaming, in Isaac's language.

I nod, my chest aching. "It's worse because he's nothing like my ex. Isaac is kind, even if he's grumpy. He's thoughtful, even if he doesn't say much. He made me feel safe, like I could be myself. He supports me and doesn't try to sabotage my success. And I threw it all away."

What have I done? I was living in a bubble where the reality of actually publishing this book didn't exist, where I could nurture my fantasy life with him without having to face the consequences. But it backfired in the most horrific way imaginable.

Christine lets out a long breath. "Look, I'm not saying it's going to be easy, but if you love him, you owe it to yourself—and to him—to try. Apologize. Tell him how you feel. Give him a chance to decide for himself if he can forgive you."

Her words make sense, but the fear of rejection keeps my heart racing. What if he can't forgive me? What if I've already done too much damage? He compared me to his ex, and knowing how deeply she wounded him, there's no way I can recover from this.

"Charlotte," Christine says, her voice firm. "You write about love for a living. About characters who overcome their fears and mistakes to find their happily-ever-afters. Maybe it's time you took a page out of your own book."

I laugh through my tears, shaking my head. "I hate it when you're right. And you know what the funny thing is?"

She shakes her head.

"He told me the same thing."

She sighs and smiles, squeezing my hand. "That's what you pay me for. Well, maybe not so much your personal life, but it's impossible to separate a writer from their feelings. So, here I am, therapist and agent." She winks at me.

I sit back, staring at my untouched coffee. Christine's right—I have to try. Because losing Isaac without even trying to fix things would be the biggest mistake of all.

For now, though, I need to sit with this feeling. To own my mistake and figure out how to make it right. Because if I don't, I'll never forgive myself.

16

ISAAC

I stand at the edge of the gravel driveway, staring at Charlotte's rental house. Her car isn't in the driveway, and the front windows are dark. Clenching and unclenching my fists as I shift from one foot to the other, I feel like a damn fool for coming here.

I prepared a speech I promptly forgot as soon as I walked out of the door. But she's the one who's good with words, not me. Especially not me. Sometimes I'll go weeks before speaking to anyone. She's right when she says I'm a grumpy hermit. I can't deny it.

But I have to fix this. I can't stay here like a creep staring at her front door.

The tightness in my chest has been unbearable

since our fight. I was an idiot for reading her manuscript, for snapping at her, especially for telling her the book is garbage—it's far from it—and for comparing her to my ex. She's nothing like her. Charlotte's...everything my ex wasn't.

And now she's probably gone for good.

I take a hesitant step toward the front door, rehearsing an apology in my head. Something about how I let my pride get in the way, how I didn't mean what I said, how I want to do anything to make up for it.

A sudden rustling noise interrupts my thoughts, and I look toward the patio. There, on the wooden bench, is the raccoon. The same one that scared Charlotte half to death when she first got here. Remembering how she climbed me like a tree is a punch in the gut.

He's scavenging again, pawing at an empty fast-food bag that someone left behind, he probably found it in the trash can down the road. For some reason, the sight of him breaks through the tension in my chest. I shake my head, a small, bitter laugh escaping my lips.

"Figures you're still here," I mutter, walking toward the patio.

The raccoon looks up, its dark eyes studying me

for a moment before going back to hunt in the bag for scraps. It doesn't even flinch when I sit down on the bench on the opposite side of the patio. Apparently, he's only scared of screaming women who aren't even tall enough to be considered a real threat. I smile at the thought.

The house looms behind me, silent and empty. I glance at the windows again, hoping to see some sign of life. A light flicking on, the sound of footsteps...anything. But there's nothing. She's gone for good. I'm too late to fix this.

I pull out my phone and stare at Charlotte's number. The screen mocks me with her name, and the last text I sent is still unanswered. Whoever invented texting should burn in hell. Just a bitter reminder that someone is ignoring you. My thumb freezes over the call button for a long moment before I press it.

The line rings. Once, twice, three times.

"Hi, this is Charlotte. Leave a message, and I'll get back to you."

Her voicemail cuts through the stillness, and I clench my jaw, fighting the urge to throw my phone across the yard. She doesn't want to talk to me, and I don't blame her. The grip around my heart tightens when I think about my speech, which I fully remember now, as if mocking me that it's way too late for that.

I sit back on the bench, staring up at the sky. The stars are faint, barely visible through the cloudy weather. The air smells like pine and damp earth, and for a second, I close my eyes, trying to imagine that she's still here, just inside the house, waiting for me to knock.

But she's not.

The raccoon finishes its scavenging and looks up at me, tilting its head as if to say, *What now?* I let out a heavy sigh and answer him, "I don't know. Do you have any suggestions?" He stares at me. I shouldn't do it. I'm the one who curses tourists for interacting with the wildlife. But right now, this raccoon is the closest I can get to Charlotte, to a memory of her. How pathetic is that?

"You're lucky, you know that?" I say quietly. "You don't have to worry about messing things up with people. You just live your little raccoon life, scavenge for food, and do your thing."

The raccoon chitters softly as if agreeing. I snort, fighting a smile and shaking my head at the absurdity of this moment.

I stare out at the empty yard, the overgrown grass swaying in the night breeze. I hated this house a few months ago, but Charlotte made it feel alive. Her laughter, her chatter, the way she always seemed to light up a room without even trying. It made me like this place. She convinced me that not all neighbors are a pain in the ass, I actually like some of them.

And I let her slip through my fingers.

I think about the way she looked at me when we first met—annoyed but curious, like she was trying to figure me out. And then, later, how her eyes would soften when she thought I wasn't looking. Like she saw something in me that I didn't even see in myself. That book told me otherwise: she saw me clear as day. I didn't have any chance to escape it. She reads people way too well not to see the cracks in their armor, except her ex-husband. On that one, she was blind.

She told me my work was art. No one had ever said that to me before, not even my ex, who always thought my woodworking was just a hobby, a waste of time, and that I was good with my hands for other *things*. But Charlotte believed in me.

And what did I do? I tore her down, accused her of using me, and threw her vulnerability back in her face.

I run a hand through my hair, the weight of regret pressing down on me. It's not just that I hurt her—it's that I lost the only woman who really saw me. Not the grumpy woodworker or the guy with a chip on his shoulder. Just *me.*

The raccoon chitters and I look at him. "Shouldn't you be scared of me?" I ask but he just tilts his head.

"You're a brave little thing, aren't you?" I chuckle softly, knowing he'll scurry away if I stand up and try to go near him. He's curious, but not stupid.

It chitters again, and I shake my head. "Yeah, I know. I screwed up big time. And now she's gone."

The words hang in the air, heavy and final. Nobody is here to acknowledge my failure except my furry friend.

I pull out my phone again, scrolling through my contacts until I find her name. My finger hovers over it, but I can't bring myself to call. What would I even say? That I'm sorry? That I was wrong? That I—

That I miss her.

The truth of it hits me like a punch in the gut. I do miss her. Her laugh, her smile, the way she'd challenge me with her wit and her fire. I miss the way she made me feel—like maybe I wasn't as broken as I thought.

The raccoon hops off the bench, scurrying

toward the edge of the patio. I watch it go, my chest tightening with every step it takes.

"Guess it's just you and me, buddy," I mutter.

But even as I say the words, I know they're not true. Because the truth is, I'm alone. Completely and utterly alone. Like she predicted with her last words before slamming the door behind her back. She saw the truth in that too.

And it's my own damn fault.

I stay on the bench for what feels like hours, the night growing colder around me. My phone buzzes in my pocket, and for a split second, my heart leaps. But when I pull it out, it's just a notification from the delivery company. Not her.

Of course not.

I stare at the empty house one last time before standing. The raccoon watches me from the edge of the yard, its dark eyes gleaming in the faint light.

"Take care of this place, okay?" I say, my voice hollow. "It deserves better than I gave it credit for."

The raccoon doesn't respond, of course. It just scurries off into the darkness, leaving me alone with my thoughts.

I turn and walk back to my house, my boots crunching against the gravel. Every step feels heavier than the last, and by the time I reach the back patio,

I'm exhausted. Has it always been so far from my house? I feel like there are miles of nothingness around me right now. No human contact to warm my cold heart.

As I sit in my kitchen in the dark, breathing in the lingering scent of her lavender shampoo, one thought keeps running through my mind: I had a chance with Charlotte—a real chance—and I let it slip away.

Now, all I can do is hope that, wherever she is, she finds someone who sees her the way she saw me. Someone who doesn't screw it up like I did.

Because I don't deserve her.

Not anymore.

17

CHARLOTTE

The bustling hum of the café around me does nothing to drown out the turmoil in my mind. I sit across from Christine, my agent, who looks unusually tense. Her perfectly manicured nails tap against the table, and her eyes narrow as she sips her latte, waiting for me to explain why I called this last-minute meeting.

I never do this. Once I deliver my book, I'm someone who dives straight into the next one. I let the people around me take care of what I can't do myself and just let the pages go and take on a life of their own.

"So?" she says finally, setting her cup down with a deliberate thud. "What's so urgent that you couldn't just email me?"

She's all business, and while I appreciate this attitude when she negotiates my contracts, I'm not thrilled to be on the receiving end of her stare.

I glance around the room as if someone might overhear us, even though we're tucked into a corner booth. My hands fidget with the napkin in front of me, twisting the paper until it's a tangled knot.

"I don't want to publish the book," I blurt out.

There. I said it. That wasn't so hard. I feel lighter and heavier at the same time. I said what I wanted to, but I also know I've let her down.

Christine blinks. For a moment, she doesn't say anything, just stares at me like I've grown an extra head. Then she laughs—a short, sharp bark of disbelief.

"Charlotte," she says, her voice low but firm. "That's not funny."

"I'm not joking," I say, my throat tightening. "I don't want to publish it. I can't."

I want to explain the million reasons I have to justify my decision, but the truth is that I feel guilty about how I treated Isaac in this book.

Her expression shifts from disbelief to concern, her brows knitting together as she leans closer. "You're serious."

I nod, swallowing hard, almost choking on my

saliva. My mouth is so parched that my tongue is glued to my palate.

"Okay." She exhales slowly, pinching the bridge of her nose. "Let's take a step back. Why don't you want to publish it? I gave it to my assistant to read, and she told me it's your best work so far. And I agree with her—it's incredible, Charlotte. The publishers will love it. The advance they gave you reflects that."

"I know," I say, my voice barely above a whisper. "It's not about the quality of the book. It's... personal."

Christine tilts her head, her sharp eyes scanning my face. "Personal? Charlotte, this is a business. You can't just decide not to publish something because it feels personal. Writing is always personal. That's what makes it good."

I know she knows why I don't want to go forward with it, but she wants to hear it from my own lips.

"This is different," I insist, my voice trembling. "I shouldn't have written those things in the first place, and you know it. I never put anything that personal and real in my books because I don't want people to know those things about me. This time, I messed up, and I'm regretting it."

Realization dawns on her face. "Is this your way of apologizing to Isaac?"

I flinch at the sound of his name, nodding reluctantly.

She sighs, sitting back in her chair, and tries to argue her point. "Charlotte, you've always drawn from your life for your books. That's part of what makes your stories so relatable. But you've also always been careful to fictionalize things. No one reading this will know it's about him. I didn't recognize him and I knew about him."

"That doesn't matter," I say, my voice rising despite myself. "I know. He knows. I recognize both of us when I reread those lines, and I can't detach from it. I can't do that to him."

Christine stares at me, her expression unreadable. For a moment, I think she might understand. But then she shakes her head, a hint of exasperation creeping into her voice.

"Do you realize what you're saying?" she asks. "If you back out now, you're not just shelving the book. You're breaching your contract. The publishers could sue you. You'll have to return the advance—and it's not like you can just write another book to make up for it. This could ruin your reputation, Charlotte. Your career."

Her words hit me like a slap, each one stinging more than the last. But it's the concern in her voice that makes my stomach curl in an unpleasant knot. I know she's right. Walking away from this book means more than just losing the money. It means losing everything I've worked for—every connection, every ounce of trust I've built with my publishers.

It's a potentially life-shattering decision, I know it too well. My whole career is on the line.

But even as she lists all the reasons why I shouldn't do it, one thought keeps rising above the noise: I can't betray Isaac like this.

"I've already decided," I say quietly.

I spent an entire night thinking about this, and the more I went through all the options, the more this one stood out like a beacon.

Christine leans forward, her voice sharp. "Charlotte, think about what you're saying. This isn't just about you. You have an entire team that's invested in this book. Editors, marketers, designers—they've all put time and effort into making this happen. Pulling the plug now affects all of them."

Guilt twists my stomach, but I don't back down. "I know. And I'm sorry. But I can't publish it. Not like this."

Everyone is counting on me, and considering the state of this industry, every published book is a miracle that comes to life. I know that a lot of people spent an insane amount of time prepping for this release, taking time away from other authors who probably deserve this chance more than me, considering I'm about to throw it away. But this is my life, the private one that I already messed up once with a nasty divorce; I don't want to screw this one up too.

Christine runs a hand through her hair, her frustration evident. "Look, I'm not saying you have to make a final decision right this second. But at least give yourself some time to think about it. Talk to a lawyer if you need to. We're talking about serious consequences here, Charlotte. This isn't just a little bump in the road."

I nod, even though I already know what I'm going to do. There's no decision to make. Not really. But I owe her at least this, considering I'm messing with her life too. Because no matter what, when one of your clients pulls a move like this, your reputation is damaged too. One more person to feel guilty for.

Christine studies me for a long moment, her expression softening. "You're not yourself," she says quietly. "I've seen you upset before—during your

divorce, when your first book risked being banned—
but this is different. What's going on?"

Tears prick at the corners of my eyes, and I look
away, unable to meet her gaze. "I hurt him," I whisper. "I did exactly what his ex did, and I did it
without giving it a second thought. And I don't know
if I can fix it."

Christine's face softens further, and for a
moment, she looks more like a friend than an agent.
"Charlotte, you're a good person. Whatever
happened, I'm sure you can make it right. You are
both adults and if he can't understand why you did
it, maybe he's not the man you think he is. He has to
give you a chance to explain, and when you do, he'll
understand."

I shake my head, my throat tightening. "I hope
you're right because I crossed a line this time, Christine. I should have been honest with him from the
beginning. I should have let him in on this project
from the very start. And I shouldn't have used our
time together to fill those pages, no matter how good
they are."

She's quiet for a moment, her gaze thoughtful.
"You're really in love with him, aren't you? I know
you already told me that, but I didn't understand the

extent of your feelings until now. This is the kind of love that makes you do crazy things."

She gazes at me with a mixture of admiration and worry. She has been with me since the beginning and has become a friend over time, which is why it was even harder to tell her this. I owe her some time to digest this news. If telling her I'll think about it will make her feel better, I can do that.

"I guess this is one of those epic stories I write books about. I didn't really understand how my heroine felt until this exact moment. Jesus, I'm really an awful author. It's no surprise my readers tell me that I rip their hearts out of their chests," I comment, and she chuckles softly, lightening the mood a bit.

Christine reaches across the table, placing a hand over mine. "Charlotte, you've always been strong. You've faced every challenge head-on, and you've come out stronger for it. You'll get through this too. But you need to be sure about what you're doing. Don't let guilt drive you into making a decision you'll regret."

I nod, even though I know there's no changing my mind. Respecting Isaac's privacy is more important than any book, any career. He trusted me, and I let him down.

Christine squeezes my hand before pulling back.

"Take some time to think it over. Call me when you've made a decision."

"I will," I lie, knowing I won't need to.

She stands, gathering her things and giving me one last look of concern. "I'll do what I can to buy you some time with the publishers. But Charlotte..."

"Yes?"

"Be careful. You're not just walking away from a book. You're walking away from everything you've built."

Her warning looms over my head like a bad omen. I went over my contract yesterday more times than I can count, and I know my future looks bleak. If I'm lucky, they'll consider our history, all the best-sellers I brought them, and let me off the hook, taking back my advance and not suing me. But that would be the best-case scenario. I don't even want to think about the worst right now.

"I know," I say softly.

She nods and walks away, leaving me alone in the café.

I sit there for a long time, staring at the untouched cup of tea in front of me. The weight of everything presses down on me—Christine's warnings, the potential fallout, the loss of everything I've worked for.

But none of it matters as much as doing the right thing.

I won't betray Isaac. Not again.

As I stand to leave, I pull out my phone, scrolling to his name in my contacts. I should answer his phone calls, or at least his texts asking if I'm in Chicago, since I left without telling him. But this is something I can't do over the phone.

If there's anything my heroines have taught me, it's that I have to look him straight in the eyes when I ask for forgiveness.

18

ISAAC

I'm staring blankly at the half-built cabinet in my living room, a project I started hours ago and abandoned halfway through. When I finally decided I couldn't stare at the coffee table in the workshop any longer, I decided to change the scenery and move in here, but now I'm staring at the couch for the same reason. There is not a single piece of furniture in this house where I didn't make love to Charlotte. Memories are everywhere, and if I'm ever going to forget them, it would be easier to just move out of this place entirely.

My tools have been scattered on the floor, untouched, for the better part of the evening. A discarded piece of wood is perched on the windowsill as if it's challenging me to remember that

I didn't spread Charlotte's leg over there to take her deep and fast.

Well, it's wrong: I took her from behind and she put her hands exactly where that board is now.

I rub my face, the frustration clawing at my chest like an itch I can't scratch. I haven't slept. Haven't eaten much either. The hollow ache in my stomach isn't from hunger—it's from regret.

The phone sits on the table, mocking me with its silence. I've called Charlotte twice, and both times, it went straight to voicemail. I didn't leave a message. What would I even say? *Sorry for being an idiot and reading your book without asking? Sorry for making you feel like you're no better than my ex?*

None of it feels like enough.

And the texts I sent? The more I read them, the more I sound like a child throwing a tantrum because she didn't tell him she was leaving. She had all the right not to tell me anything after how I treated her.

A knock at the door cuts through the heavy silence. For a second, I wonder if I imagined it. Then the knock comes again.

I get up, my heart pounding for reasons I don't want to think about too much. It's probably Henry stopping by to check on me again. He's done that a lot lately. I must really look pitiful if he's come to my house personally to check on me. Or maybe it's some random delivery I forgot about.

But when I open the door, it's none of them. It's Charlotte.

She's standing there, looking up at me with those wide, vulnerable eyes that knock the air right out of my lungs. Her hair's loose and wild around her face, and she's clutching her duffel bag like it's the only thing keeping her grounded.

"Hi," she says, her voice soft but steady.

For a moment, I can't say anything. I just stand there, staring at her like an idiot, wondering if this is real or some cruel trick my exhausted brain is playing on me. I've imagined meeting her again so many times I can't tell if this is another one of my vivid dreams.

"Are you going to let me in?" she asks, raising an eyebrow. There's a smile tugging at her lips, like she's trying to suppress it. Well, that's encouraging.

"Yeah," I say, stepping aside. My voice cracks, and I clear my throat, trying to pull myself together. "Yeah, of course. Come in."

She walks past me, her sandals clicking softly on the wooden floor. I close the door and turn to face her, my heart hammering in my chest. Now that she is here in front of me, I forgot everything I wanted to say. My brain seems reluctant to catch up with the reality of her presence.

"I wasn't sure you'd want to see me," she says, her voice hesitant.

Why would she think something like that? I'm the one who messed up.

"I wasn't sure if you'd ever talk to me again," I admit.

She lets out a shaky laugh. The sound is tinged with something that makes my chest ache. "Well, here I am."

She sounds like she doesn't know what to say either. We didn't have a chance to talk about our "situationship"—as Henry informed me the young people like to call it these days—and now things are even more complicated.

We stand there for a moment, the silence stretching between us. It's not uncomfortable, but it's heavy, loaded with everything we haven't said yet.

Finally, she takes a deep breath and says, "I'm not publishing the book."

Her words hit me like a punch to the gut. This was definitely not what I expected her to say. "You are an asshole" was my top option, followed by

"You're going to have to crawl if you want my forgiveness," but definitely not this.

"What?" I ask, frowning. "Why?"

"Because I understand now," she says, her voice firm. "I understand how much you value your privacy, how much you trusted me. And I betrayed that trust. I can't publish it, Isaac. Not if it means hurting you."

Her words send a wave of relief crashing over me, so powerful it nearly knocks me off my feet. I take a step closer to her, my hands trembling at my sides. But not because she's not going forward with the publication—that is an insanity we have to discuss—but because she's doing it to avoid betraying and hurting me.

"Charlotte," I say, my voice breaking. "You didn't have to do that. You didn't have to give up your book for me."

It seems I can't say anything more than that, even though my brain is in turmoil with all of the things I want to spit out right now.

"Yes, I did," she insists. "Because you're more important to me than any book. More important than my career. I love writing, but I don't love it more than I love you."

If someone had told me three single words could

kick all the air out of my lungs, I would have laughed. Hard. But here I am, trying to fill my lungs with enough oxygen to function.

I don't think. I just move.

In two long strides, I'm in front of her, pulling her into my arms. I hug her so tightly it's like I'm afraid she'll disappear if I let go. I've missed her presence so much it physically hurt.

She stiffens for a moment, then melts into me, her arms wrapping around my back. I bury my face in her hair, inhaling the scent of her—lavender and a hint of something else that is entirely *her*.

"I'm so sorry," I whisper, my voice raw. "I'm sorry for everything I said, for the way I acted. I never should have read your book without asking. I never should have made you feel like you were like her. You're nothing like her, Charlotte. You're... everything. And you're a great writer, and your book is not garbage. It's fantastic. I mean, I'm not an expert or anything, but I know art when I see it."

She lets out a choked sound that sounds like a mixture of a sob and a laugh. She pulls back just enough to look up at me. Her eyes are glassy with unshed tears, and she bites her lip like she's trying to hold them back.

"You're forgiven," she says softly. "But you're still an idiot for reading my book without permission."

I laugh, the sound rough and choked. "I know. I deserve that."

I deserve so much more, but I am determined to make up for it. Not with words, those aren't enough.

She studies me for a moment, her gaze searching mine. "Did you really like it?" she asks, her voice almost shy.

I shake my head, and her face falls. Before she can pull away, I cup her face in my hands, forcing her to look at me.

"Charlotte," I say firmly, "it's the most amazing book I've ever read. You have to publish it."

Her brows knit together, confusion flickering across her face. "But—"

"No buts," I interrupt. "You're a writer. A damn good one. That book deserves to be out in the world. I was just too stubborn and stupid to see that at first. Publish it. Change the world with it. I was just shocked you could see so deep into my soul that I recognized a part of me I wasn't ready to face yet."

Tears spill over her cheeks, and she lets out a choked laugh. "You're really okay with it?"

"More than okay," I say. "I'm proud of you."

And I really mean it. That novel has so much love in it; it would be a shame to keep it hidden from the world. It should be taught in school to show kids what it means to love someone so much you *see* them. In a world full of screens and phones that give us such a distorted reality, what we really need is to be seen.

She throws her arms around my neck, pulling me into another hug. I hold her close, feeling like I can finally breathe again.

When she pulls back, her gaze drops to my mouth, and my breath catches.

"I missed you," she whispers.

Before I can respond, her lips are on mine, soft and warm, and everything I've been craving since the moment she walked out my door. She breathes the life into me that's been missing since she left.

I kiss her like a starving man, pouring all the emotion I've been holding back into the press of my lips. She responds just as fiercely, her hands entangled in my hair as she presses against me.

We stumble back toward the couch, our movements frantic and uncoordinated. I barely manage to sit down before she's straddling my lap, her lips never leaving mine. One of the tools I tossed aside earlier is pressing hard against my lower back, but I don't care. The only thing that matters is her body against mine.

Her hands tug at my shirt, and I help her pull it over my head, tossing it aside. She then traces a line of kisses down my neck, her touch leaving a trail of fire in its wake. I've missed those lips so much.

I return the favor, slipping the sundress over her head and basking in the exhilarating sensation of her shivering skin under my fingers.

"Charlotte," I murmur, my voice low and rough.

"Shut up," she whispers against my ear, her breath hot and teasing, making the hair on my neck stand.

I chuckle, my hands gripping her hips as she grinds against me. "Bossy, aren't you?"

"You love it," she says, her tone smug.

She's not wrong. This is what I missed the most. Our banter, her way of bringing out the talkative side of me, the one I'd locked up in a corner of my heart when my ex broke it. I didn't realize how much I've changed over the years until Charlotte stumbled —or better, climbed— into my life and showed me how I used to be.

I flip her onto the couch, pinning her beneath me. Her eyes sparkle with mischief and something deeper, something that makes my chest ache in the best way. She said it out loud before, but the love I read in her eyes is a whole new level of affirmation.

"I do," I admit, leaning down to kiss her again. "And you know what else I love?"

She shakes her head, waiting for an explanation. "You. I love you." I look right into her eyes, enjoying every single shade of surprise that lights them up.

The rest of the world fades away as we lose ourselves in each other. There's no more doubt, no more fear—just us, tangled together on the couch, finally finding our way back to each other.

EPILOGUE
CHARLOTTE

The bookstore buzzes with conversation, low chuckles, and giggling. The scent of freshly brewed coffee mingles with the sharp tang of new hardcovers. A long line of readers snakes through the aisles clutching copies of *Falling for the Grumpy Neighbor*. Their faces are lit with anticipation, and some of them tiptoe to better see me behind the tower of my brand-new book.

My heart flutters in my chest. I will never get used to these book tours promoting a new release. Sure, I know what to expect. I'm not nervous about messing up, but the energy buzzing through me never goes away. It's part of the thrill of being a writer.

I sit at the signing table, a Sharpie in one hand

and a smile plastered on my face. My cheeks ache from hours of smiling, but I'm not complaining. This is a dream come true. Meeting my readers is just as exciting as the first time. The difference now is I can enjoy it more because I don't feel like I'm going to throw up any minute.

Isaac leans against the wall to my right, arms crossed, watching me with an expression that's equal parts amusement and pride. He's dressed in his usual faded T-shirt and ripped jeans, his hair gathered up on his head in a messy bun, looking every bit like the grumpy hero readers have fallen in love with. Even though he'd never admit it, I know he's happy when women throw glances his way. But the best part is he only has eyes for me.

A young woman steps up next, her eyes wide and sparkling. She's clutching her book so tightly I'm worried she'll crumple the cover. She's wearing a yellow summer dress, like the woman on the cover. She's not the only one; I've seen quite a few during this tour, and every time, I'm amazed that people identify so closely with one of my characters. Something that never ceases to thrill me.

"Hi!" she says, her voice breathless. "I just wanted to say I love your book so much. It's my favorite romance of all time. Not that I don't like your other books, but this one feels special." She stumbles nervously on her words and I smile.

My heart swells, and I beam at her. "Thank you so much. That means the world to me."

She hesitates, glancing over her shoulder at the line behind her before leaning in and whispering, "Can I ask you something?"

"Of course," I say, uncapping my Sharpie.

"Where did you get the inspiration for the story? I mean, it feels so real. Like, were you writing about a real person?"

I'm often asked this question. In the beginning, I was reluctant to expose myself, but then Isaac told me to just be me... This book is just like that: *me*.

I laugh, the sound coming more naturally than I expected. "Well," I say, my voice teasing, "let's just say I did a bit of method writing for this one."

And let's leave it at that, because "he fucked me silly" is a bit rude to say out loud.

Her eyes widen. "Method writing? Like, you really had a grumpy neighbor?"

"Something like that," I say, glancing at Isaac. His lips twitch, trying to hide a smile, but he doesn't interrupt. "When I was working on the book, I kind of...well, I sort of broke into my neighbor's house."

The crowd around the table erupts into laughter,

and the woman gasps, her hand flying to her mouth. "You broke in?"

She looks shocked. And I would be too if someone just admitted they'd committed a crime.

I nod, biting back a grin. "It was an accident —sort of. I needed a change of scenery to help me write, and his house had this incredible view of the woods. I thought no one was home; the door was open, so I let myself in to soak up the inspiration. Turns out, someone was definitely home."

Everyone gasps and chuckles. Quite a few interested ears perk up from the back of the line.

"Did they call the cops?" another fan calls out from the line, their voice filled with mock horror.

I glance at Isaac again, his smug smile now fully formed. "No," I say, turning back to the crowd. "He didn't call the cops. But he did give me a piece of his mind."

I roll my eyes, remembering that day and how the grumpiness came out of him in full force. Sometimes, we still laugh about what he told me, that he thought someone broke into his house to make coffee.

"And?" the young woman presses, her curiosity shining brighter than ever.

"And now we live together in that very house," I say, my voice softening. "We're very happy."

The crowd lets out a collective *aww*, and Isaac rolls his eyes, though the corner of his mouth quirks up in a smile he can't hide.

The woman looks between us, her grin stretching from ear to ear. "That's the most romantic thing I've ever heard."

"See? It happens in real life too!" I tell her, signing her book.

"But don't break into your neighbor's house. It's still a crime, even if you write a book about it," Isaac chimes in, making everyone laugh.

And this is one of the things I love so much about him. The way his funny side shines through when you least expect it.

I finish signing her book and hand it back. "Thank you for reading," I say sincerely. Then, she walks away, clutching the book to her chest like a treasure.

The next few fans come and go, their excitement infectious. Eventually, there's a lull in the line, and I take a moment to stretch my fingers and sip some water.

Isaac steps closer, his voice low enough that only

I can hear. "You're really telling people you broke into my house?"

I look up at him, feigning innocence. "I mean, it's not a lie." I tease him the way I used to in the privacy of our home.

His eyes narrow, but there's no heat behind it. "You're impossible."

"And yet, here you are," I say, grinning.

The next fan approaches. He's a middle-aged man with glasses perched on his nose. He flips his book open to the title page and slides it across the table. "You said you broke into a house for inspiration," he says, his tone curious. "Do you think it was the place that made the book so good? The setting?"

I pause, the Sharpie frozen an inch above the page. This is the first time someone has asked me something like this. They usually stick to the book, not how I created it.

"No," I say slowly, my thoughts drifting to when I was writing it. "It wasn't the place. It was the warmth of the person who lived there."

The man raises an eyebrow, and I glance at Isaac again. His expression softens, and he looks away, pretending to inspect a nearby shelf. Some things will never change, and I smile.

I return my attention to the fan, smiling. "For a

long time, I thought I needed a special space to write. After my marriage ended, I couldn't write anything good. I blamed it on losing my office, on not having the right setup. But that wasn't it at all."

I sign the book, my handwriting steady despite the emotion welling up inside me. "It was that my home didn't feel like a home anymore. The warmth was gone. And no matter how beautiful the house, it's the people who live in it that make it special."

The man nods thoughtfully, taking his book back. "That's a beautiful sentiment," he says.

"Thank you," I say, watching as he walks away.

When the line finally gets smaller and the signing comes to an end, I lean back in my chair, letting out a sigh of relief. These signing sessions are as exhausting as they are exciting. Isaac steps forward, holding out my purse.

"Ready to go?" he asks.

I take it, smiling up at him. "Yeah."

The brisk evening air wraps around us as we walk out of the bookstore together. I glance at Isaac, his profile strong and grounding beside me.

"Do you ever think about how crazy this all is?" I ask.

"Which part?" he says, his tone teasing. "The

part where you broke into my house, or where you turned it into a bestselling novel?"

I laugh, bumping his shoulder with mine. "All of it. I never imagined my life would look like this."

"Neither did I," he admits, his voice softer now.

We walk in silence for a while, and the sound of our footsteps is the only noise on the quiet street. I never thought a man—my man—would support me so fiercely in my career, let alone come with me on a signing tour. But here I am, with Isaac escorting me like the gentlemen he is.

When we reach the car, he opens the door for me, his hand brushing mine as I slide inside.

As he gets in and starts the engine, I look at him, my chest tightening with a warmth I never thought I'd feel again.

"I've never been this prolific in my life," I say suddenly.

He glances at me, one eyebrow raised. "What do you mean?"

"I mean, I don't even have an office anymore," I say, laughing. "I write at the kitchen table, or on the couch, or wherever there's space. But I've never been able to write so much, so easily. It's like the words just...flow now."

He doesn't say anything for a moment, focusing

on the road. Then he reaches over, his hand finding mine.

"Maybe it's because you're finally home," he says quietly.

I squeeze his hand, my throat tightening. "Yeah," I whisper. "Maybe it is."

~

Thank you so much for joining me on Charlotte and Isaac's journey in *The Grump and the Writer*! I hope their love story brought a smile to your face, a little swoon to your heart, and maybe even inspired you to avoid raccoons at all costs.

If you enjoyed this book and want to be the first to hear about my upcoming releases, special surprises, and behind-the-scenes fun, be sure to subscribe to my newsletter! You'll get all the juicy details delivered straight to your inbox.

https://wendyashford.com/newsletter/

Let's keep the love and laughs going!

ACKNOWLEDGMENTS

Writing a book is like climbing a tree—it's messy, unpredictable, and occasionally involves a raccoon. Thankfully, I didn't have to do it alone.

First, to my editor, Staci, the true magician behind the scenes. Thank you for taking my rambling drafts and helping me transform them into a story worth reading. Your brilliance, humor, and ability to spot plot holes from a mile away are nothing short of heroic. I owe you endless gratitude...and probably a bottle of wine.

To my husband, who puts up with my chaotic, snack-fueled writing marathons and pretends not to notice when I "borrow" his hoodies for inspiration. You're my partner in crime and the steady hand that keeps me grounded—when I'm not climbing you like a tree in my imagination.

And, of course, to my four-legged writing assistants. To my dog, who kept my feet warm while loudly auditioning for the role of a chainsaw, and to my cat, who sat on my keyboard just enough to almost delete the entire manuscript. Your "help" will never be forgotten (though I'm still finding stray fur in my laptop).

Finally, to you, the reader, thank you for picking up this book and joining Charlotte and Isaac on their wild ride. I hope it made you laugh, swoon, and maybe even want to climb a tree yourself—preferably without a raccoon involved.

ABOUT THE AUTHOR

Wendy Ashford loves to write spicy small-town romance novels that end with a Happily Ever After. She lives in the Pacific Northwest with her husband, dog, and cat. She loves the beach during winter and walking in the snow.

She likes to read, play with Legos, and watch romantic comedies on Netflix when not writing.

Follow her on social media:

facebook.com/wendyashfordbooks

instagram.com/author_wendy_ashford

ALSO BY WENDY ASHFORD

The Grump and the Chef

www.ingramcontent.com/pod-product-compliance
Ingram Content Group UK Ltd.
Pitfield, Milton Keynes, MK11 3LW, UK
UKHW021035260125
454178UK00001B/15

9 798230 975021